Books by Deb Brammer

Peanut Butter Friends in a Chop Suey World

Two Sides to Everything

Moose

MOOSE

Deb Brammer

Greenville, South Carolina

Library of Congress Cataloging-in-Publication Data
Brammer, Deb, 1954-
  Moose / by Deb Brammer.
      p. cm.
  Summary: High school student Moose is a new Christian and pretty rough
around the edges when he joins his friend Cody in the Montana wilderness
for an unforgettable week at Moose Creek Bible Camp.
  ISBN 978-1-59166-722-3 (perfect bd. pbk. : alk. paper)
  [1. Camps—Fiction. 2. Christian life—Fiction. 3. Montana—Fiction.]
I. Title.

PZ7.B735788Moo 2006
[Fic]—dc22

                                                           2006031548

Design by Nathan Hutcheon
Composition by Sarah Kurlowich
Cover Photo Credits: iStock International Inc. ©2006 (sky, foreground);
Unusual Films (boy)

ISBN 978-1-59166-722-3
15   14   13   12   11   10   9   8   7   6   5   4   3   2   1

To all our friends in supporting churches
in western Montana.
Your friendship and support
have meant so much over the years.

Contents

1

Moose leaned over to pick up the soccer ball. A pack of cigarettes fell out of his shirt pocket. The girls searched for something to look at in another direction. Pastor Steve, our youth leader, eyed me as if to say, "Cody, do something!" I rolled my eyes. Moose put the cigarettes back in his pocket, oblivious to all the awkward glances he was causing.

One more thing to talk to Moose about. No more cigarettes at youth group.

The ball rolled in from the sidelines. Danielle and Lindsay passed it down the floor. Hannah tried to steal it, but Danielle used surprisingly agile footwork and defeated her plan. She passed it to me. I sent it to Lindsay. She faked a pass to me and kicked it back to Danielle. These girls were getting better.

Soon all our feet were squabbling for the ball, wondering whose foot would win the argument. Suddenly Moose's big cowboy boot came down hard on Danielle's heel and settled the issue. Danielle crumpled, and with her, the rest of us fell like a line of dominos. My glasses slid across the floor.

Danielle shrieked in pain. "Those huge boots of his should be outlawed! They're lethal!"

Pastor Steve sighed. "You've got to be more careful," he told Moose.

Moose shrugged. "You said to be more aggressive."

I rescued my glasses, stood, and looked up into his unrepentant face. "I think he was talking to the girls."

Our little youth group in Hungry Horse, Montana had grown to six girls and me—and now Moose. The last thing we needed in our group was a more aggressive Moose. It was a safety hazard to have him play at all.

But Moose was a miracle. I had to keep telling myself that.

When Moose wore his cowboy hat in church and spoke out during the service I told myself, "Moose is a miracle."

When he told jokes with racial slurs at church, I reminded myself again.

For five years I'd been the only guy in our youth group. Now I finally had a Christian friend who didn't talk about crafts and hairdos and nail polish. Moose was rough, a bumbling bull moose in a church full of bunny rabbits, but he was my friend.

At school all the other guys drank and partied on weekends. Since I didn't want to do that kind of stuff, I had no other school friends. I worked with elderly ladies making huckleberry shakes at the ice cream shop. Nice as they were, they weren't going to hunt or fish with me. So Moose became my best friend, my only guy friend. Somehow Moose and I were going to make friendship work.

Pastor Steve decided we'd had enough soccer. We moved on to refreshments. Since Moose started coming to youth group Pastor Steve always made sure the girls went first. Not only was this common courtesy, it was his way of making sure the girls got something to eat.

Moose loaded his plate with chips and cookies and grabbed a glass of Coke. He clomped over past where Danielle was sitting.

"Hey, Danielle," he said over a cheek full of food. "Sorry about your foot."

"It's all right," she mumbled. "It'll heal—sooner or later."

An apology. That was progress.

I crunched tortilla chips and picked up the brochure for Moose Peak Bible Camp. Pastor Steve had handed it to me before youth group. I had always loved going to Bible camp. This year I'd be taking my new miracle friend with me. Maybe camp would give Moose a good boost to his Christian life.

I flipped the brochure over to the camp rules. No smoking. No drinking. No firearms. No swearing. I added a few more items to my mental list of things to talk to Moose about. I had some work to do before Moose was ready for camp. I never knew a miracle could be such a problem.

Moose didn't look like a miracle, act like a miracle, or smell like a miracle. But he was.

It all started last September in shop class. Mr. Erickson told us to choose partners for the year. When everyone else had teamed off, two were left—huge, obnoxious, foulmouthed Moose Richards and me—Cody Boedecker. At almost eighteen, I had given up on the growth spurt Mom promised me. I was one of the few guys in the entire school who actually went to Sunday school. From my straight brown hair to the sport shoes I never outgrew, I was average and unremarkable. That was OK with me. After all, my main goal at school was to be invisible.

I ignored Moose's foul language. On Mondays when he bragged about how much booze he drank at parties, I changed the subject. When he asked what I had done for the weekend, church never came up. I thought about witnessing to him or inviting him to church, but when you talk about lost causes, I decided Moose was a legend.

Then one Monday Moose looked worse than normal. His curly blonde hair lay in uneven clumps, and his eyes looked more red than their usual green.

"What's wrong?" I asked. "Hangover?"

Moose silently sorted through the tool box.

"Sometimes I wonder if it's worth it," he said.

"If what is worth it?"

"Drinking. When my stepdad, Bill, drinks, my mom suddenly develops new bruises. I hate that beast! Then Saturday night I drank all night long. I woke up Sunday morning on our front porch, face down in the bushes. Who knows what I had done the night before? Could have been anything."

What could you say to something like that?

"Well," I said. "You could quit, you know."

3

Mr. Erickson started giving instructions then, and I never said any more about it. Weeks later I noticed he had quit bragging about his parties on Monday morning. Then a few weeks after that, on a day Moose was absent from class, Mr. Erickson said, "I heard Moose quit drinking."

I almost dropped my jig saw. "Really? What made him do that?"

"He said you told him to quit."

That was the first miracle. All I had said was five words. *You could quit, you know.* But when I thought about all his friends and family, I decided that I must have been the only person who ever suggested the obvious.

When Moose quit drinking, he lost all his drinking buddies. He seemed kind of lonely, so I invited him to come to church. Miracle number two happened. He came.

About a month later the third miracle happened. Moose got saved! I couldn't believe it. Who would think Moose Richards would ever pray the sinner's prayer?

But the third miracle was far from complete. Moose was born again, but he was still a baby Christian. Even the cutest baby is less than inviting in dirty diapers. As a baby Christian, Moose was no more appealing than a dirty baby.

Moose had quit drinking. He only smoked when he was nervous. He didn't swear as much as he used to. But he was about as tactful as a grizzly bear. I felt like the park ranger trying to make peace between the grizzlies and the tourists.

"Look out Moose Peak," I murmured. "Here I come with my miracle friend."

For several weeks I searched for ways to sneak suggestions into our conversations that would prepare Moose for camp. He had agreed to go. Someone had anonymously donated his camp fees. With a little help from me he'd be ready. Thankfully most of the campers had been Christians a while. They would have to be patient with Moose. But some things Moose would just have to change.

I caught him smoking in town one day. "What's with the cigarette?" I asked.

Moose shrugged. "Stuff is going on at home. Mom is threatening to leave Bill—which is hard to do when he's living in her house. Thankfully she was smart enough to keep the house in her name when she married him. But it's kind of hard to make him move out when he's bigger than I am. Just the usual stuff. Nothing new."

"Sorry about that. It must be hard for you."

"Part of life I guess. Haven't had a cigarette for a week and a half. Just needed one to get me through."

If he hadn't smoked for a stress-filled week and a half, maybe he could get through an easy week of camp. Then I reminded myself that camp wouldn't be as easy for Moose as it was for me.

"You can't smoke at camp, you know."

"I know. I understand the no smoking rule. But it seems like they'd take it easy on a smoker who's trying to quit."

"I think they sympathize with someone who's trying to quit, but they just can't allow smoking at camp. I mean, they want to help, but they just can't allow that."

"Maybe I'm not ready for camp."

I almost choked on my gum. "Sure you are. You've got to go to camp."

"Why?"

"Because . . . because, well, camp is just what you need right now."

"How do you know?"

"I've been to camp, and it's fun, and it always helps me a lot. Anyway camp is a good place to go when you're trying to quit smoking. No one else will be smoking, and you can't buy cigarettes. It's perfect."

"Maybe." Moose glanced at his cigarette, then tossed it to the ground and ground out its spark with the heel of his boot.

"Well, isn't it?"

"I suppose you're right."

I dared to breathe again. Moose had to go to camp. He had gotten off to a fairly good start in his Christian life. He had come to church every Sunday and every youth group for four months. Yet I knew that a lot of the sermons were over his head. Our

5

little church in Hungry Horse couldn't offer big youth programs and special speakers. Camp offered one solid week of Christian friends and spiritual help aimed just at our level. This was our last chance during high school for this kind of spiritual encouragement. Who knows where Moose would go after that?

I only hoped camp would help Moose like it had helped me. Last year at camp I told the Lord I would be a missionary. Two months later I became Moose's woodworking partner. Now I was his friend. Somewhere in between he had become a Christian. I never quite figured out how, but somehow God had used me in the process.

We had jumped the smoking hurdle. Then one day Moose's truck got stuck in the mud, and he let out a cuss word.

I cleared my throat. "Excuse me?"

"What? Did you belch or something?"

"No, but you still need to work on your language."

"Oh, yeah. You said I couldn't say that word anymore. But I don't get it. I didn't say God's name. I've worked really hard not using God's name as a cuss word anymore, and I almost never do."

"That's a start. But some of those other words are offensive to Christians. It's not a good testimony to unsaved people either."

"So what am I supposed to say?"

I was ready for this. "Buzzard."

"Buzzard?"

"Yeah. Like the bird. *Buzzard* has a certain ring to it, don't you think? And it won't offend anyone. So whenever you start to say a cuss word or bad word, just say buzzard instead."

"So buzzard is my own personal Christian cuss word?"

I shrugged. I'd rather think of it as a nonoffensive answer to an offensive problem. "Who knows? Maybe it'll catch on."

"You're sure camp is worth all this?"

"Yes, it is. Besides, you need to give up cussing as much as you need to give up smoking."

I thought everything was settled until a few days before camp. Moose met me after work. We grabbed huckleberry shakes and drove Moose's truck to a pretty little spot by the Flathead River.

6

Water rushed over boulders, under logs, and around bends. We tossed rocks in the river and watched the tourists drive by.

"So." I said. "Just a few more days until camp."

Moose fired a rock downstream and knocked a twig off a boulder. "I don't know. Maybe I'll give camp a miss this year."

No. Not after all the work I'd done to prepare him. Not when he was just starting to grow as a Christian. "What do you mean you'll give it a miss?"

"Think I won't go."

"Why not? Someone already paid your way. The food's pretty good. You like kayaking and fishing and stuff. We play games and shoot targets and pull pranks."

Moose's eyes lit up. "Pranks? Like what?"

Perhaps I had said too much. "Oh, you know. Just the typical camp pranks. Like sneaking up on a sleeping person, squirting shaving cream in his hand, and tickling his nose."

"Is that all? Can't you come up with something better than that?"

"The pranks may be simple, but they're harmless and that is really important at camp. You can have fun, but you can't hurt anyone. There are lots of fun things to do at camp. Come prepared to have a good time."

"I don't know."

"Why don't you want to go?"

Moose sorted through the rocks at the river's edge. "Well, I got to talking to Jack at the gas station the other day. He's a Christian, but he doesn't go to church. He says he can worship God better fishing by a lake than he ever could in church. Makes a lot of sense to me."

No. This could not be happening. "Sounds like an excuse to me. Do the fish preach to him and tell him how to live for God? Do the trees encourage him to do what's right?"

"Maybe he reads the Bible on his own. At least he doesn't have hypocrites in the church to distract him."

I hurled a rock at a fallen log, hard, and hit it dead center. "That's the oldest excuse in the world for not going to church. That is so lame. Why should I take it out on God because some

7

Christian isn't doing the right thing? Besides, our church people are nice. They're not perfect, but you and I aren't perfect either, are we? Christians need each other. That's part of the reason God tells us not to forget to get together with believers in church."

"Yeah? What verse is that?"

"I don't know, but it's there somewhere."

Moose gathered a handful of pebbles and tossed them one by one into the river. "Church is good for you, Cody. You grew up in church, and you know how to act. I'm sure camp is the highlight of your social calendar. But I'm just not a team player."

"What does that mean? You're going to quit going to church and skip camp?"

"I might go to church once in a while. But you'll get along at camp much better on your own. Believe me."

"But Moose, you've got to go to camp!"

"Why?"

"Because. You got saved. You quit drinking. OK, not in that order, but you did. You quit smoking . . . almost. You quit swearing. You're beginning to learn stuff about the Bible."

"Right. My Bible knowledge is amazing!"

"You learned a lot about Samson in Sunday school."

"Samson's OK. I like when he tied the foxes' tails together and let them loose in the cornfields."

"See? That's a start. You still have a lot to learn, but you're going in the right direction. Church can help with that. And camp is good. It's not all preaching. You'll have a lot of fun too. And there are all these Christians our age. At school there are practically no Christians, and everyone is trying to get you to drink and party and listen to dirty stories. But camp is different. Where else are you going to find that many Christians our age?"

"I just think camp would get along better without me. I don't fit in like you do. Like church and youth group. When I first got saved everyone was all happiness and congratulations. But now people look at me like I'm about to pick their pockets."

Were our church people growing impatient with Moose's problems? I supposed they were. And Moose was right in a way. At camp I could relax and fit in. But Moose couldn't relax. He would have to struggle to fit into camp and do what Christians expect.

Camp would be easier without him. But I'd had eight good and easy years of camp. This year I was not going for myself. I was going for Moose. He had to go.

I tossed a pebble at a floating leaf and hit it. "Look. Don't worry so much about the others at camp and what they'll think. People will understand that you are a new Christian and learning about stuff. Christians care about each other. They expect new Christians to make mistakes. There are some rules, but really it's just common sense. When you try to please the Lord and be nice to other people, you will automatically do most of the stuff you're supposed to do."

"Love God and be nice."

"Exactly. You do that, and you'll get along just fine at camp."

Moose kicked some rocks into the river. "Maybe, maybe not. But I think I'll just give everyone at camp a break and not make them figure out what to do with me. It'll be much nicer for everyone if I'm not there to ruffle any Christian tail feathers."

"No. That is definitely not true. Church and camp were never meant to be places to just show off the wonderfulness of good Christians. I mean Christians should have a good testimony, but church is there to help people. Saying you shouldn't go to church because you might mess things up—that's like going to a hospital and telling the sick people to go home because they're giving the hospital a bad reputation."

"So now I'm a sick person?"

"So now you're not perfect. Now you need to grow. Like me. I need you at camp."

"Right. You couldn't get along without me."

"Moose, you're the best thing that happened to me this year! Last year at camp I told God I would be a missionary. But I had never told anyone outside of church about God. You know me at school. I'm invisible. No one cares about what I say. But God gave me a miracle this year. You're my miracle."

"Oh, yeah. I forgot. I'm your missionary project. If I don't turn out right, you fail the course."

9

"It's not like that. OK. Maybe it's kind of like that, but it's not only that. I mean it was exciting for me to see you get saved, and I pray for you to grow in the Lord like nothing else. But you're my friend too, the only one I've got. OK, so I'm not Mr. Popular. I still need you."

"Not at camp you don't. You keep telling me about all these Christians at camp. Make one of them your camp buddy."

"But Moose, they're not you. You ask the hard questions. You make me think about what I believe. You keep me real. I mean, I could be a hypocrite and get away with it around the others, but not you. You're sure to point out every flaw. Now who else is going to be honest enough to do that?"

Moose snorted. "Mom would be glad to know I'm running for the honesty award."

"Look. I know it's hard. The newness of being saved has worn off, and now you're trying to change. That's not easy, but you've got a good start. You can't give up now."

"I'm not giving up. I'll talk to God on my own. You and I can still be friends. If you're an angel in the Christmas Pageant, I'll come see the show."

I was losing this battle. If I lost the camp battle, next would be the church battle. Before long Moose could be drinking with his old buddies again. I was desperate.

"No. Wait. Just give it a chance. Five days of camp. Give it your best shot. Give the others at camp a chance to be friends. Give God a chance to speak to you. Just . . . just let camp be camp and see what happens. I think a week at camp will show you that Christian teaching and Christian friends are totally worth the trouble."

Moose pulled a log into the river and pushed it into the current. I knew Moose. He was thinking. He would answer when he was ready and not before.

"OK. I'll make a deal." He wiped his hands on his jeans. "If I finish a week of camp, and go away feeling it was worth it, then I'll give church another try too."

"Good."

"But that's only my side of the deal. If after camp I've had enough of camp and churchy things, you have to promise to quit bugging me about going to church anymore."

Oh. I should have known there was a catch. Still, if he was losing interest in church now, my bugging him wouldn't make much difference.

At nine thirty light still hung in the summer Montana sky, but the shadows on the cliffs reminded us daylight was quickly slipping away. My miracle was slipping away too. Moose had only begun to change. It would be easier for him to slip back into his old habits than continuing to fight to make new ones. He still felt awkward in the world of Christians. And I knew what happened to Christians who thought they didn't need church and the Bible. They might be nice people like Jack at the gas station, but they never became strong Christians.

Should I push him to go to camp? If I promised not to nag him about church, I'd have to stick to it.

I stuck out my hand to Moose. "It's a deal," I said.

He shook my undersized hand with his oversized one. "Deal."

2

Little David had to fight huge Goliath. That was hard. But what if David, instead of fighting Goliath, brought him back to the Israelite's camp and made them play games together—for a whole week. I imagined David would feel just about like I did bringing Moose to Bible camp.

Monday morning our youth group piled into the van and drove to camp. The girls chattered about important things like toenail polish. Moose and I sat in the back staring at the scenery, wriggling like caged animals ready to spring loose.

The trip passed quickly, and we were soon unloading. I brought my usual small sports bag. The girls had two bags a piece with their make-up and outfits and girlie things. Moose had a surprisingly big bag too. But this was his first year. He had obviously brought a lot of stuff he would find out he didn't need.

As the van pulled into the parking lot, Wesley sauntered over to greet us. Wesley W. Walters. For some reason I never got close to Wesley last year. He didn't exactly seem like my type. Maybe it had something to do with the fact he had lived most of his life in Sweetwater, Tennessee. But his dad was a pastor in Great Falls now, and Wesley had been saved for practically all of his life. Maybe he could help me with Moose.

As Pastor Steve pulled the bags out of the van, I introduced Wesley to Moose. Dark-haired, skinny Wesley could look blonde Moose right in the eye. "Moose just got saved this year," I said.

"So now it's two of us guys against our six youth group girls. I guess the Lord knew I needed some help."

Wesley stuck out his hand to shake Moose's—like a pastor or something. "Welcome to Moose Peak Bible Camp," he said.

The girls claimed their luggage and headed for the dorm. Wesley, ever helpful, grabbed Moose's bag. He got kind of a sideways grip on the handles, and a cigarette pack with several cigarettes fell out.

Wesley's mouth fell open. "What are these cigarettes doing in your bag? You can't bring cigarettes to camp. It's against the rules. Besides, smoking is sin."

Moose set his sleeping bag down and snatched the cigarettes. "They're just backups, in case I get desperate."

"I don't care what they are," Wesley said. "You can't have them at camp. My dad's the camp dean. He'll tell you."

Moose sighed. "Look. I just quit smoking. I hardly smoke at all. But when I get really nervous, I still need one. I won't use them unless I absolutely have to. OK?"

Wesley folded his arms. "No, it's not OK."

Pastor Steve walked up behind us with a sleeping bag under each arm. "There's Pastor Mac. He'll want to meet Moose."

Pastor Steve had great timing. Maybe later I could catch Wesley alone and explain about Moose.

I waved at Pastor Mac. "His last name is McKenzie," I explained. "But everyone calls him Pastor Mac."

Pastor Mac carried a suitcase in each hand and two under his arms. His hair might be graying, but he hadn't slowed down any.

He set down the suitcases and shook Moose's hand. "Welcome to camp, Moose. We're really glad you could come. Pastor Steve told me you have become a Christian this year."

Wesley spoke up. "He brought cigarettes with him. He can't have cigarettes at camp. Tell him, Pastor Mac."

I said, "He's trying to quit."

"If he's trying to quit, why did he bring cigarettes to camp?" Wesley asked.

Pastor Mac leaned against the dusty van. "I think Moose understands we don't allow smoking at camp. I'm glad to hear you're giving up the habit, Moose. I used to smoke before I was a Christian. I gave it up, but it wasn't easy. I kept going back to it for several years, but it felt so good when I finally quit. Stick to it. You'll get there."

Wesley stared at the cigarettes in Moose's hand. "But what do we do with the cigarettes? Should I give them to my dad?"

Pastor Mac held out his hand. "I'll take care of those for you," he told Moose. "You guys just go on up to the dorm and get settled. I think we're going to have a great week of camp."

Moose glanced one last time at his cigarettes and placed them in Pastor Mac's hand. Moose let go of the cigarettes like a drowning man losing grip on a life preserver.

Moose and I settled into the dorm and walked around a bit. We kicked a ball around the soccer field and waded in the edge of the lake. At noon we hung around the dining hall. I introduced Moose to some of the counselors and Morris Moose, the moose head camp mascot that hung over the serving window. Lunch was Sloppy Joes. Moose ate three. At least he liked the food.

Let's get started, I thought. *Tell us what we're going to do this week.*

Last year we had a lot of time to hang around and go kayaking and fishing on our own. The year before, however, we were busy every minute playing some trendy new youth group game. I hoped for Moose's sake that this year would be simple.

Pastor Steve stepped to the front of the serving window just below the head of Morris Moose. "Eureka!" he shouted. He almost bounced with energy. "Who can tell me what *eureka* means?"

Nathan Wilder from Kalispell yelled out, "It's a town just north of here."

"Right. It also means, 'I found it!' Or it can mean 'You don't smell too good.' But this week Eureka means we're going to have a great time. Eureka is one gigantic game with lots of parts. Now you may think that Montana is never mentioned in the Bible. But this week we're going to do some Montana Bible sports and find all kinds of Montana things in the Bible. If you're not good at one thing, you'll be good at something else. Everyone adds something to the team. The secret for winning Eureka is teamwork. The more each person participates, the better your team will do."

Great. And Moose wasn't a team player. I had to keep my eye on him to make sure he didn't run for the door.

"Friday night the winning team gets their choice of pizzas from Maria's Gourmet Pizza in Whitefish, plus huckleberry pie and ice cream for dessert.

"Second place team gets ordinary pizza. Third place gets their pick of the leftovers for the week. They have to empty the trash cans Saturday morning before they leave camp. Fourth place gets whatever leftovers the third place winners don't eat. They have to sweep out the chapel and dining hall before they leave. Fifth place gets beanie-wienies, and they have to pick up litter. And sixth place winners . . ."

Pastor Steve paused for dramatic effect. What could be lower than beanie-wienies?

"The team in sixth place gets to eat the cook's best peanut butter and jelly sandwiches. To them we give the honor of cleaning the dorm toilets before they leave."

Pastor Steve divided us up into six teams of six players each. Each team had an animal mascot. We were the Grizzlies, and Pastor Steve made me the captain.

I had never been captain of anything in my life. It must have had something to do with a talk I'd had with Pastor Steve after prayer meeting about a month before. "I'm confused," I had told him. "I think the Lord wants me to be a missionary, but I'm not much of a leader. I'd rather just do what I'm told. I'm just not much of a speak-out, stand-up-front, tell-everybody-what-to-do kind of guy. Do you think I got this missionary idea all wrong?"

Pastor Steve smiled. "You sound a lot like Moses at the burning bush. God isn't finished with you, Cody. He's still working on all of us."

"So how do I learn to be a leader?"

"By leading."

I guess I asked for it.

Besides me and Moose, the Grizzlies were: Wesley W. Walters, now from Great Falls; a red-haired chatterbox named Montana (Tana) Atkins from Polson; Titus Haider from Missoula; and

Meadow Red Owl from Browning. It was Meadow's first year, but she looked familiar.

Pastor Steve dismissed us to meet down at the lake. Moose was the first one out the door. I had to run to catch up to him.

"So camp is going to be one gigantic game," Moose complained. "Perfect. All week long I have to buddy up to five team members."

"Give it a chance. You're great at fishing and kayaking. Who knows? If you're not careful, you might have fun."

"Fat chance of that."

"Come on. Don't knock it before you've tried it. We don't have to win, just finish well. My dad always says even if you don't win, you can hold your head up high if you finish well."

"And if we finish last, you still win our bet, and I have to go to church. Plus we get this stupendous award of PBJ sandwiches and the toilet cleaning honor. Great motivation!"

"Hey, it's just a game. Moose Peak has the best camp food around. Thursday nights we always have barbecued elk steaks, and Mrs. Johnson cooks them better than anyone I know. So what if we do lose? One meal of PBJ sandwiches won't kill us."

"We'd still have to clean the toilets."

"So? You've gotta remember this is a small church camp. It's less expensive than bigger camps because we rely on volunteer labor. Every year they assign the campers cleaning duties before we leave. This year Pastor Steve just divided it up by teams. If it comes to that, it won't kill us to clean the toilets. Our moms do it all the time, and they don't complain."

"Mine does. Which reminds me. I've got to go to the little boys' room."

"So go already. Or do you want me to go with you?"

"Hey, what do you think I am? A girl? I can go by myself."

Moose jogged towards the restroom. I took the opportunity to snag Wesley.

"Hey Wes, I need your help."

"Fine. But call me Wesley. I was named after John Wesley, and I don't like to see his name demeaned."

"Good for you. Hey, last year didn't you say you wanted to be an evangelist when you grow up?"

"That's right. I've already preached several times for my dad. And I pass out tracts every Saturday at the mall."

"Great. I've got a project for you. Moose is a new Christian. He comes from a really rough background, so camp is all new for him. He really is trying to do the right thing, but it's not easy. He doesn't really feel like he fits in yet. I thought maybe you could help me out."

"Sure. I can watch him and make sure he doesn't do anything wrong. Maybe I could show him how to take sermon notes."

Now I remembered why I never got close to Wesley last year. I'm all for being spiritual, but it was like Wesley never learned to relax.

"No, no, no. Not that. Just be a friend. You know."

"Got ya."

I doubted that. I knew what I was asking, but what did Wesley think I was asking? "Pastor Mac is a good speaker," I said. "So I think we can leave the preaching up to him. You know, just be nice. Help Moose feel a part of things."

"Hey, I got it. Trust me."

Trust him. Wesley was already Mr. Gung-ho Gospel, off to change the world. I'd just handed him a license to start preaching at Moose. What was I thinking?

We had arrived at the lake, and Moose was catching up to us. Three kayaks stood ready by the shore. Our team grouped together.

I glanced at the kayaks, the water, and Pastor Steve. I cleared my throat. "OK, Grizzlies. Three double kayaks and a stopwatch. I think that means we'll have to paddle out to those buoys and back, three teams at a time, two people at a time. Let's work together. There's lots of events, so don't worry if we don't win this first one. Just do your best."

"That's right, Grizzlies. Listen to your captain." It was Luke I'm-better-than-you Sutherland—the Coyote captain. If I had known how hard this year was going to be, maybe I wouldn't have challenged Luke eight years ago. "You don't have to win," he said. "Just do your best."

I worked up a smile. "Hi, Luke. Nice to see that you could make it."

Luke rubbed his hands together. "You didn't think I'd miss this year, did you, Cody? Can you believe this is our ninth year of camp together? Every year we compete, you and I, and every year we come in about even. But last year you waved goodbye to me, and what was that you said?"

"See you next year?"

"Oh, yes. You said that all right. But what was that other part?"

"I guess I said I looked forward to beating you this year."

"Yep. That, too. 'Winner takes all,' you said. 'Whoever wins this year is the camp champion.' Isn't that right?"

"I guess so. But it's not just you and me this time. We have our teammates to think about."

"That's right, Captain Boedecker. This year we'll see not only how well you compete, but how well you lead. This should be interesting—unless you're scared and want to back out?"

I glanced at Tana, who had just popped a big bubble of gum. Wesley was tall but, if I remembered right, terrible at sports. Moose was strong but hopeless at Bible games. After eight years, however, I could hardly back down now.

"Better tell your Coyotes to watch out for the Grizzlies!" I said.

Luke strutted off.

Moose studied my face. "What was that all about?"

"Never mind. Just do your best."

"Cody is right," Titus said. "We have lots of events. We aren't going to win them all. But we have to keep going hard. We have to make sure we don't get too far behind. Even if we come in third or fourth place on some events, we can make it up by coming in first in events where we have strong skills."

Pastor Steve blew his whistle to get everyone to quiet down. "Jesus and his disciples spent a lot of time boating across the Sea of Galilee. Paul and his missionary friends also sailed across the

Mediterranean. So boating is a great Bible sport, which we also love in Montana. For our first race we're going to divide into twos and race kayaks out to the buoy and back. Three teams will race first, then the other three. I'll time you."

I told Pastor Steve we'd go with the second set of teams. That would give me a chance to figure out what a captain was supposed to do. I sized up my fellow Grizzlies. Wesley and Moose were about the same height. Sandy-haired Titus was short like me. But the girls might need some muscle in their kayak. Tana had been to camp for years and could talk to anyone. Meadow, however, was new to camp and hadn't made friends yet.

"Maybe two of us guys should team up with the girls and help them out," I suggested.

"I'll go with Moose," Wesley offered. Good, Wesley. Just be a friend.

"OK. Titus, why don't you go with Tana, and I'll go with Meadow."

"We have to move together," Titus told Tana.

"I know." Tana moved her arms in a rowing motion. "It's like pompom girls doing a cheer."

"I was thinking more of a three-legged race," Titus said. "But you have the right idea."

Titus and Tana talked over some moves while the rest of us cheered for the first three teams. When it was our turn, Titus and Tana agreed to go first. They got in the kayak and waited for the starting signal.

Pastor Steve fired the starter's gun. The teams began paddling. Titus and Tana worked together and made pretty good time. They were second in line, just ahead of the Coyotes.

"Go Coyotes! You can beat those miserable Grizzlies!" Luke yelled.

"Don't listen to them, Grizzlies," I shouted. "We can beat the Coyotes any day." I forgot Luke and turned to Meadow. "Do you know how to paddle a kayak?"

Her dark eyes twinkled. "I think I can handle it."

19

Calm. Confident. Somehow I could picture her running. Now I knew why she looked familiar. "You run cross-country, don't you?" I asked.

She smiled.

"You're the fastest girls' runner in Montana's class A schools. In fact the coach in Columbia Falls thinks you can outrun most of the runners in the AA schools."

She shrugged. "God made me fast. I enjoy running."

The Antelopes and Coyotes made it back to the shore and were changing places. Titus and Tana paddled in next. Meadow slipped into the kayak behind Tana, and I took Titus's place.

Meadow grasped the paddle and plunged it into the water. I matched her move. Steady, strong strokes brought us well out into the water. I watched her, matched her, worked to keep up with her. Straight, black hair swept past her shoulders in perfect rhythm with each practiced stroke. Pure poetry. And I had offered to help this Native American learn how to kayak. What an idiot!

I laughed. "Guess you enjoy kayaking too."

"I do."

"Awful nice of me to help you out like this since you're just a girl, huh?"

She laughed. "Don't know how I'd get along without you."

We rounded the buoy about the same time the Antelopes did, then passed the Coyotes.

I glanced over at Luke in the next kayak. "Better watch out," I said. "You'd hate to be beaten by some miserable Grizzlies."

"Ooh. I'm scared," Luke answered.

We pulled up to shore. I rolled out of the kayak to make room for Moose.

"We're in the lead now. Go for it!" I yelled.

Moose stepped in easily and sat down. Wesley grabbed the side of the cockpit closest to him, then planted both feet close to his hand. The kayak began to roll, but Moose leaned the other direction, balancing the kayak until Wesley got settled. Wesley sliced into the water with one end of the paddle and then the other, straight up and down, like slicing butter with a knife.

"Not like that," Moose yelled. "Use the broad sides of your paddle, but push the water with your paddle as you bring it up."

Wesley tried again. This time the broad sides went in, but barely skimmed the top of the water.

"You need to plunge the paddle deeper," Meadow said. "Steady and deep."

Wesley worked some more and the two of them finally moved out into the water.

"Go Grizzlies!" Titus yelled.

Tana joined in. "Think huckleberry pie!"

Moose tried to match Wesley's rhythm but Wesley's uneven strokes were hard to match.

"We've got to work together." Moose yelled. "One . . . two . . . one . . . two."

But no matter what Moose did, Wesley's paddle seemed to hit the water on the half beat. So much for our lead. They must not go kayaking much in Sweetwater, Tennessee. Thankfully, some of the other kayakers hadn't had much experience either, but by the time Moose and Wesley hit the buoy they were in last place.

And they did hit the buoy—literally. Moose deepened his strokes on the buoy side of the kayak, maneuvering the turn. Meanwhile Wesley thrashed around, dipping the paddle in everywhere. Just as they were about ready to straighten out, Wesley's paddle glanced off the heavy buoy, knocking it out of his hand.

Moose stopped paddling while Wesley reached for the paddle. Waves formed by a passing motor boat washed the paddle out just beyond Wesley's reach. Another wave brought it closer, but as he reached out it slipped away from him again. Each wave teased him, bringing the paddle a little closer, then farther. Wesley made one frantic reach for it, and the kayak rolled. Both guys plunged into the water just as the Antelopes pulled up to shore.

Moose rescued the paddle. He rolled himself back into the kayak, which was no easy task. With angry strokes he paddled to shore, leaving Wesley to swim. Stroking with his life jacket and a full set of clothes, Wesley was splashing like a pre-schooler.

"Try standing up," I called to Wesley. "The water's not that deep."

"Oh," he mouthed. He stood and walked to shore, dripping from head to toe.

Luke sauntered over. "Looks like the Grizzlies aren't so fierce after all."

By the time our kayak reached shore some of the teams had walked away, but Pastor Steve hurried over to meet them. "Way to finish, guys."

Moose rolled his eyes. "Well, I guess we could have just stayed out in the water."

"You guys were really starting to get the hang of it before you capsized," Tana chattered. "If you could do it all over again, I think you'd do just fine. I mean, a lot of people were having trouble getting the kayak started. You should have seen some of the Mountain Goats getting around their buoy. Too bad the kayak rolled."

"Really," I said. "You finished, and that's good. We came in last this time, but we'll do better next time. With six teams, every team will be good at different things, so we won't be stuck in last place for long."

"Cody," Moose growled.

"Yeah?"

"Shut up."

Moose was right. There was a time for a leader to lead and time for him to keep his mouth shut. This once, I knew exactly what to do.

3

Evening brought chapel time. Time for business. Chapel was the reason I had begged Moose to come to camp. I had gambled Moose's future church attendance on chapel. Pastor Mac was the camp speaker. Since Pastor Mac was born and bred in Montana, Moose could relate to him if he could relate to anyone.

We Grizzlies sat on some folding chairs on one side near the front. I sat on one side of Moose. Wesley sat on the other.

We sang some lively choruses. I was anxious for the sermon to begin, but first we had to continue our team competition.

Pastor Mac announced that we'd be digging for gold. Actually gold digging was a fancy name for a Bible drill. Normally I liked Bible drills. I wasn't the best at them, but I was far from the worst. However, with Moose along, I dreaded it more than any other part of camp.

Pastor Mac stood at the front, leaning on the somewhat crooked podium. "Psalm 19 tells us that God's Word is more to be desired than gold," he said. "When we read it, it's like digging up treasure. When I say 'shovels up,' hold your Bibles over your heads. When I say 'dig,' you can start looking. When you find the verse, put your finger on it, stand up, and name the metal or precious stone that the verse mentions. I'll have a question for the second person."

Wesley glanced over at Moose who was holding his Bible about shoulder high. "You have to hold your Bible up above your head," he whispered. "And you have to hold it by the back, by the spine."

"Why?"

"So you don't cheat. If you hold it by the spine, you can't mark a place with your finger."

"Shovels up." Pastor Mac eyed each group to make sure everyone was ready. "Look for the stone that the body was made of. Daniel 10:6."

We repeated the reference.

"Dig!"

We all began to hunt. Wesley stood up so fast he almost knocked his chair over. "Beryl," he called. Fifty points for the Grizzlies.

A Coyote popped up next.

"What metal were the arms like?" Pastor Mac asked her.

"Brass." Twenty-five points for the Coyotes.

When everyone had found the verse, we read it, closed our Bibles, and held them up again.

Next came 1 Samuel 17:7. Iron was the metal. Goliath's spear was made of iron. Fifty points for the Coyotes and twenty-five for the Grizzlies.

Wesley sat down and leaned over to Moose. "You started before he said dig," he pointed out.

"So?"

"You can't do that. It's cheating. Do you want to lose points for our team?"

Moose looked over at me.

I shrugged. "It's the rules."

Moose was always the very last one to find the verse, so I didn't think it mattered that much. But Wesley was right. Technically it was cheating.

Several more verses were found and read. I came in second once, even though my mind was distracted by Moose and his constant struggle to find the verses.

"Look for the stone that is polished," Pastor Mac told us. "Lamentations 4:7."

Wesley was first again. "Sapphire." Then he spotted Moose running his finger over the names of the books in the index.

Wesley whispered furiously, "You can't look in the index. That's cheating."

"But I don't know where Lamagination is," Moose whispered back.

"It's Lamentations."

"Right. Page 834."

"You can't look it up by the page number. That's cheating. Plus, the whole point of a Bible drill is to know where the books are so you don't have to use the index."

"How am I supposed to know where they are? When I became a Christian, was I supposed to just suddenly be granted the knowledge of Bible book order?"

"No. You have to work at it. You might try memorizing them."

"I don't think I'll get that done in time to finish this Bible drill."

"Look, you already made me miss the last two references. Our team was leading until you started using the index!"

I was never so glad to have a Bible drill finish. We sang a couple of songs while Pastor Steve tallied up the points for the first day. Wesley had lost the kayak race for us, but he had made up for some of it with the Bible drill. Too bad the Bible drill wasn't worth as many points as the kayak race.

Pastor Steve uncapped a marker and stepped over to the mascot pictures on the chapel wall. "In last place we have the Antelopes with 225 points." He wrote "225" under the antelope picture. At least we weren't in last place.

"Keep working Antelopes. There's lots more events. You can catch up. Second to last are the Grizzlies." He wrote "250" under the grizzly bear. Titus pumped his fist into the air in a half-hearted cheer. "Go Griz."

Mountain Goats had 350; Bobcats—450; Eagles—575.

"In first place at the end of day one of Eureka we have the Coyotes with 775 points. Let's hear it for the Coyotes!" Pastor Steve led the cheering.

Luke looked at me and whistled. We clapped politely.

The Coyotes would be hard to beat. Actually I wouldn't mind who else we beat as long as we beat the Coyotes. Rivalry could be fun, but this year it only complicated things. If I had known about Moose last year, I certainly wouldn't have challenged Luke. "Next year's winner is the champion!" What an idiot! I wasn't even a competitive person when Luke wasn't around. Why did I let his jabs get to me?

We sang one more song before the sermon. I told my mind to shift to spiritual things. After all, that was the whole point of camp.

Pastor Mac dressed like a logger and treated you like one of the guys. I prayed that he would say something that would help Moose. He began, however, with a situation that had confused me about God for years.

"You remember a couple of years ago when we got that hard winter?" Pastor Mac leaned on the pulpit, propped one boot on the bottom, and searched the eyes of each camper. "Cars and trucks wouldn't start. Pipes froze and kept the plumbers busy. We skipped spring entirely. The only people with smiles on their faces were snowblower dealers."

Several campers whispered back and forth. Everyone in Montana had a story to tell about that winter.

"Animals had a hard time too. Some starved." Pastor Mac straightened. He fumbled with his notes. "But who can forget the biggest tragedy of the winter? Evan Blake."

I couldn't forget. Evan's dad worked with my dad. The family was still a mess.

"Evan was building a snow fort where he could play with his friends. He didn't mind the long winter. He loved to tube down the hills and build snowmen and play in the snow. But while he was playing, hidden in the trees, a hungry cougar watched his every move. Suddenly the cougar sprang from the trees and knocked Evan over, breaking his neck. Evan died instantly."

Was Pastor Mac going to explain why God let that happen? I hoped so, but his sermon took a different direction.

He cleared his throat and eyed the audience once more. "The Bible says Satan is like a roaring cougar, like a mountain lion stalking his prey, seeing who he can devour. Some call cougars ghost cats because they can live quietly, invisibly, among people, watching their every move. When you are walking in the woods, a cougar could be watching you, and you'd never know.

"Camp is a great place. But Satan, the great Ghost Cat, is still hiding in the trees, stalking you. How can he make you sin?"

He leaned on the pulpit again. "Well, Satan could tempt you to rob a 7-Eleven or get drunk and spray graffiti all over the chapel, but no. That would be obvious. Satan is more likely to tempt you with little things. He wants you to criticize your team members and blame them for making your team lose. He wants you to complain about the food and hate the activities. Or maybe he tempts you to feel superior to those who complain about the food and the activities."

Preach it, Pastor Mac. The kayak race wasn't exactly the best start for our team.

"Just remember Satan is hiding in the trees, stalking you. You need to watch out. It's not hopeless. You can always do right no matter how Satan tempts you. Even if everyone else is doing wrong, you can always do right."

I copied that last sentence. I wanted to use it with Moose sometime. Then I pulled my multi-tool out of my pocket and used the ruler to underline the sentence.

No wonder it was so hard to live for the Lord sometimes. I could almost sense Satan hiding in the pine trees behind camp ready to attack. A very quiet group left the chapel that night.

By the time we played a few games and had a late night snack, however, most of the campers had shaken off their cougar fears. As Moose and I walked to the dorm, Ryan and Nathan came running out the door with Wesley's striped pajama pants in their hands.

Moose watched them zip by. "What are they up to?"

"They're probably going to run Wesley's pj's up the flag pole."

"Why?"

I shrugged. "Tradition, I guess. People feel like they have to pull pranks at camp. I don't know why. Most of these pranks have been done so many times, they're not really funny anymore."

Moose's eyes lit up. "We ought to do something! What kind of prank could we pull?"

"Maybe we ought to save our energy for the contest. Gourmet pizzas and huckleberry pie sounds pretty good."

"Come on, Cody. There must be something we can do."

"Tell ya what. If you think of a really good prank, a funny one that doesn't make anyone mad, you tell me. Until then, I pass."

"You're no fun."

"Maybe I'm just mature. We're the oldest guys at camp. We could stand to be mature."

Just then Pastor Steve stuck his head in the door. "Where's Nathan's suitcase?" he whispered.

We showed him where it was.

"Nathan and Joel have identical navy T-shirts, but Nathan's a lot bigger. Joel said I could switch shirts. Then when Nathan finds his shirt a little tight, I can tease him about all the food he's been eating."

Moose laughed. "You're really going to do that?"

"Why not? He pushed me off the dock last year."

Pastor Steve made the switch and sneaked out of the room.

Moose scowled at me. "So, Mr. Maturity, if pulling pranks is such a bad idea, how come Pastor Steve does them?"

I frowned. "I think we can trust Pastor Steve to be mature enough to pull appropriate pranks. I still think I'll pass. There's enough stuff to do without that."

Moose looked disappointed, but he let it drop.

"Hey, what's the deal with you and Luke?"

I sighed. "Well, it all started eight years ago at junior boys' camp. Luke was the tallest boy there, and he thought he was the moose's antlers."

"I'm taller than he is."

"Yep. But he got his growth spurt early, and you know how it is in fourth grade. Tall is everything. Of course, I was the shortest kid at camp. That didn't bother me. I've always been short. I make up for it in coordination. Luke's growth spurts made him

28

clumsy. I could beat Luke most of the time at dodge ball . . . and box hockey and soccer."

Moose laughed. "Kinda tough when you're the tallest kid to be beat by the shortest."

"Exactly. Luke would sing, 'Zacchaeus was a wee little man,' to me. I'd sing, 'Only a boy named David,' to him. He goes to a big church in Missoula. He'd make fun of our little church in Hungry Horse. I'd tell him why small churches were better than big ones. Years went by, but we were always on opposite teams at camp. It really bugged him when he found out I could beat him at basketball."

"Ouch."

"He had height on his side, but I could outmaneuver him. We were fairly evenly matched, but somehow I usually ended up winning. After a few years it became camp tradition to see which of us would win. I didn't really care that much, but everyone else did. I had to make a decision. I either had to lose on purpose so Luke would forget about it, or I had to absolutely cream him."

"You creamed him."

"Nope. Barely beat him. Every year it's the same. Neither of us can win decisively and put it to rest. The whole camp expects us to compete. We couldn't stop now if we tried."

"So he's the big bully, and you're the little underdog?"

"No. Luke isn't mean, just competitive. We like to think we're the best of enemies. This is our last year at camp. Last year I stood like an idiot by the camp gate as he was leaving and said, 'One more year, Luke. Whoever wins next year is the champion.' "

"So you've got to win this year."

"This year I wish I could relax and not worry about it. But I was the one stupid enough to make the challenge. I can't really expect him to forget about it."

"You could pull a prank on him!"

I passed. This year would be complicated enough without getting that started.

I taught Moose the survival tips for living at camp. Open all doors slowly and carefully. Carry Kleenex with you in case the doorknobs are greasy. Check the toilet seats for plastic wrap. Smell the contents of your shampoo bottle before you use it. At least the pranks were predictable. We got the same ones every year.

Getting Moose through his first day of camp had exhausted me. I persuaded our room to go to sleep early. When I woke up, I took the usual precautions alert for pranks. The worst I found, however, was "hi" scribbled on the bathroom mirror in soap.

Moose was still in the shower when it was time to leave. I called out to him that I was leaving and shuffled away to breakfast. Dr. Walters met me at the door to the dining hall.

"Cody, I need a word with you. Do you know anything about the salt in the sugar bowls," he asked.

"What do you mean? Did someone put salt in the sugar bowls?"

"Just answer the question, please."

"I have no idea what you're talking about."

"I need you to be sure, Cody. I saw Moose leaving the dining hall early this morning before the cooks were even in the kitchen."

"So maybe you ought to ask him about it. I don't know anything."

Dr. Walters scratched his head. "You two do almost everything together. You're quite sure you don't know anything about this?"

"I don't. Honest." I held up my right hand like I was swearing on the Bible. I waited with Dr. Walters at the door, wishing Moose would hurry up.

A few more campers straggled in. Moose came in last. Dr. Walters called him to one side.

"The cooks found salt in the sugar bowls," Dr. Walters said. "Do you know anything about that?"

Moose shrugged. "Who me? I'm not the cook."

"Do you want to tell me why you were leaving the dining hall early this morning?"

Moose glanced at me for help, then back at Dr. Walters. A nervous grin split his face. "Hey. Everyone else was pulling pranks."

I closed my eyes, shutting out this new problem. Why did I have to be such a heavy sleeper? I couldn't watch Moose twenty-four hours a day.

Dr. Walters did not smile. "One of the cooks was making coffeecake. She didn't want to open a new bag of sugar, so she used what was in one of the sugar bowls. Now they'll have to throw out all the coffeecake they made for breakfast. You may have thought your prank was innocent, but because of what you did the whole camp will only have corn flakes for breakfast today."

Oh. So we wouldn't be eating that wonderful coffeecake I smelled.

Moose ducked his head. "Oops. Sorry. I never expected the cooks to use it. I just thought someone would put salt on his cereal, and it would taste nasty, and he'd make a funny face."

Dr. Walters rubbed his head like it ached. "It's not funny to waste food. Plus the cooks have enough to do without having to put up with shenanigans like that. You are going to have to face consequences for your actions."

Moose shrugged and walked away. We headed for a table, but Dr. Walters grabbed my arm. "Cody, I know Moose is a new Christian, but we can't start making exceptions to all the rules just for Moose. If these pranks get out of hand, the whole week of camp becomes miserable. Moose is your friend. You brought him to camp. So you're going to have to keep your eye on him. Help him understand what kind of behavior is expected at a Bible camp. I expect you to keep anything like this from happening again."

I opened my mouth to say it wasn't my fault if Moose did something while I was sleeping. Was I my brother's keeper? Then I remembered—I was exactly that. It wasn't fair, but I was his friend. It was my job.

4

When Paul wrote, "Do all things without murmurings and disputings," he must have been thinking about great tribulations like Tuesday morning's breakfast. A constant murmur joined the steady crunching during breakfast. I couldn't blame anyone. With the smell of Moose Peak's famous coffeecake in the air, corn flakes tasted like cardboard.

"Corn flakes aren't even worth getting up for," Ryan grumbled. "Last year they had extra stuff every morning."

"Well, Moose ruined that, didn't he?" Wesley said.

"You mean this is Moose's fault?" Ryan asked loudly. "Thanks a lot, Moose!"

Whispers rippled over the dining hall. Nothing stayed secret for long at camp.

"Look," I said. "Moose didn't mean to ruin the coffeecake. He was just pulling pranks like everyone else. Only his backfired."

Everyone at our table gave us dirty looks.

"Young people, may I have your attention, please?" Dr. Walters stood straight and tall in front of the serving window. Ryan pointed to Morris the Moose. Someone had added a blob of hot glue to his lower lip. Morris appeared to be drooling just above Dr. Walters' head.

Giggles and whispers broke out across the dining hall. Dr. Walters glanced up to see where the attention had shifted. He smiled weakly and took a giant step sideways.

He shook his head. "Only in Montana. Listen, young people. Pranks seem to be an inevitable part of camp. I've never figured out why. But I expect y'all to use some common sense about this. I will have zero tolerance for pranks which damage property or hurt anyone. This morning one camper's prank ruined the breakfast coffeecake. This action wasted food, our cooks' time, and deprived the whole camp of a nice breakfast."

"It was Moose," Wesley announced.

Dr. Walters glared at his son. "I don't think we need to mention names, but this is a good reminder to all of us that though a prank may seem funny, we need to consider possible outcomes before we go ahead with it. Since this is the first violation of this kind and I feel that the camper did not understand the damage his prank would cause, we will be lenient. I warn y'all, however, that the consequences for another prank of this magnitude will be much more severe."

After announcements Dr. Walters informed Moose that he would be on dish duty for the entire day. "And, Moose," he said, "I expect you to apologize to the cooks for the trouble you've caused."

"Don't worry about it," I told Moose. "I'll help with the dishes."

As much as I hate doing dishes, I wanted to soften the blow for Moose, though the punishment could have been much worse.

Moose and I headed for the kitchen. Inside, three cooks stood side by side waiting for us. I recognized Mrs. Johnson from Polson. I thought the other two were from Kalispell. I nudged Moose.

"What?"

"Now's your chance. Apologize."

"Oh. Yeah. Hey, I'm sorry about the salt," he mumbled. "I didn't think it would cause such a problem."

Mrs. Johnson smiled at Moose. "You're Moose, aren't you? You're from Hungry Horse."

"Yeah."

She waited until Moose made eye contact with her. "I hear you've been saved recently."

"Yeah."

"That's great, Moose. Let me explain how things work at Moose Peak Bible Camp. We're volunteer cooks. We don't get paid. We try to have nice meals for the campers. We try to choose things we think you'll like. We also have smart campers. They've figured out that no good prank passes the kitchen door."

"Yeah. It's hard to figure out what people are going to think is funny here."

"I can understand that, so I'll tell you. Moose drool is funny. Messing with the food is not." She turned toward the sinks. "Now Dr. Walters tells us you guys want to help with the dishes. Even though the coffeecake didn't turn out right, we still have all the dishes for it."

Mrs. Johnson dressed us up in plastic aprons and ran steaming hot water in the huge camp sinks. Moose washed and rinsed. I dried and figured out where to put things.

Moose scrubbed on an enormous cake pan. "Guess I didn't make any friends with my sugar bowl prank, huh?"

"Nope."

"You'd think we were on a wanted poster the way people look at us. I thought you said Christians have a sense of humor."

"Well, like the cook said, people don't like you messing with their food."

Moose worked the metal scrubber into the corners of the pan getting the last bits out. He rinsed it and set it in the drainer. "Anyway, I did the crime and you're getting punished too. That's not really fair."

I shrugged. "What are friends for?" I hunted out the storage place for the big mixing bowl. "Some day we'll laugh about this. I know you didn't mean to ruin the coffeecake. The prank just got away from you. Pranks have a way of doing that. That's why I didn't want to pull any. You've got to make sure when you plan a prank that you don't hurt anyone and you don't destroy any-thing."

"Like pj's up the flagpole?"

"I guess. Actually the Moose drool was good. No one ever thought of that before. When in doubt, ask your good buddy Cody who is now patiently doing the time for a crime he didn't commit."

He worked the dishrag between the wires of the mixer beater. "Yeah, well, I guess I owe you one for helping me work off my debt to humanity."

I would settle for being able to sleep at night.

As soon as we finished the dishes it was time for Esau's Quest. Since this event took place in the archery field, it was pretty obvious what we'd be doing.

The Grizzlies gathered and headed toward the archery field. I was captain, but I had spent so much time worrying about Moose, that I had neglected the others. I noticed Titus was wearing a T-shirt with some pretty intimidating wolves on it.

"Hey, Titus," I said. "Nice T-shirt."

He stopped, faced our direction, and held out his shirt. We all stopped to read it.

"Save the wolves?" Moose coughed. "Is that supposed to be a joke, or are you a tree-hugger or something?"

Titus met his glare, never moved, never blinked. "I love trees," Titus told him evenly. "I think we need to save our wolves and our forests."

"And I think we need to save our jobs," Moose bellowed. "You environmentalists are putting Montana out of work. What are the loggers supposed to do when they can't feed their families? Starve?"

"I don't want anyone to starve, but I think we need to respect our environment and leave something for the next generation."

"Well, my stepdad is a horse logger, and I work with him. We go into those sensitive areas where crazy environmentalists won't allow big rigs. So don't talk to me about respect for the environment." Moose shook his finger in Titus's direction. "If you'd let loggers thin out our forests, we wouldn't get such destructive forest fires that burn whole mountainsides. If you really want to protect our forests, you ought to let the loggers do their jobs!"

Silence hung in the air like a huge stormcloud threatening to burst. Titus' eyes locked onto Moose's. Neither wanted to blink first. I don't think Titus wanted a fight on his hands, but he wasn't about to back down either. Moose, on the other hand, didn't mind a fight at all.

What now?

Meadow's gentle voice sliced through the silence. "We all love Montana and want to keep it beautiful," she said. "Moose, you know how to fell trees with a minimum amount of damage to the environment. My dad's Blackfeet. He teaches me a Native American respect for nature and how to use it responsibly. And Titus, if you live in a wood house, you must also believe in using the resources God gives us responsibly."

Titus shrugged. "I never said we shouldn't use any wood. But we shouldn't endanger our forests just to provide luxuries either."

Meadow's eyes met those of Titus, then Moose, gently challenging them to set aside their differences. "Well then, I think we are all thankful for the natural resources God has provided."

Thank you, Meadow. First poetry in motion, now quiet reason defusing an emotional bomb. She might even have something more interesting to talk about than nail polish and hairdos. Pastor Steve should have made her captain.

The rest of the team had begun to walk again, however. I had to hurry to catch up. We found the archery field and gathered downfield from our target.

Pastor Steve gave basic instructions. Each player got five shots. The bull's-eye was worth twenty points. The last outer circle was worth two. After the kayak disaster he had decided to give us some practice shots before shooting for points.

Jeremy, a counselor from Kalispell, handed Meadow the bow and arrow. She raised it shoulder high. She pulled back the string and fired an arrow straight to the yellow center of the target.

"Good shot!" Pastor Steve exclaimed.

"Everyone in my family is a big bow hunter. I shot my first antelope with a bow." Meadow laughed. "But my Bible knowledge isn't so good. We'll have to count on Wesley for that." She handed the bow to Tana.

We all took turns drawing back the heavy string, firing, missing the target completely, hitting a few shots.

Moose's first shot nicked one side of the outer white circle. "Buzzard!" he roared. "Give me a .22, and I'll do better. My brother and I shot so many squirrels on our property that the dogs had nothing left to chase."

Titus rolled his eyes. "Now there's something to be proud of."

"Really. I can shoot the tail off a squirrel at fifty yards. Isn't that right?" Moose looked to me for confirmation. "Cody and me did a little target practice just last week. I must have got me fifteen squirrels. Cody didn't do too bad either, did ya Code?"

Meadow's big brown eyes found mine and waited for an answer. I turned away only to find Titus staring at me. Last week squirrels had honestly seemed like no more than running targets, practice for game that would feed our families. Today, however, with two pairs of eyes boring into me, I felt like I'd shot the president.

Moose pulled back the string and let another arrow fly. "My brother and me found a logging trail once that had loads of squirrels. If you want good target practice . . ."

"Moose, shut up." I muttered. We didn't even use those words in my family, but with Moose jabbering away dangerously I didn't have time for the "please be quiet" routine my Mom suggested.

"What?"

"Just shut up, that's all. You've said enough."

Moose handed the bow to Wesley and looked around the group. He eyed Titus. "Don't tell me I've offended our team's tree-hugger."

Meadow broke in. "Actually, I don't think any of us are vegetarians. God told Noah that animals were given to man for meat." She eyed me. "But I don't think that includes target practice."

Titus pumped his fist in a little cheer. "Amen to that."

"OK, that's enough practice," Jeremy said. "Let's shoot for real."

We each took five shots. Tana came last. Her arm shook as she pulled back the taut string. During practice she had missed the target more than she had hit it. She held the string close to her nose, released it, and sent one shaky shot right to the edge of the center yellow circle.

"Wow!" Moose said. "That was a lucky shot."

Wesley put on his best preaching voice. "There's no such thing as luck."

Tana grinned. "Thanks for the compliment, Wesley. If it's not luck, it must be skill."

"What do you mean, there's no such thing as luck?" Moose asked.

"Well, God controls the universe. Nothing happens by chance. If Tana hits the target, that's not luck, that's God's blessing."

Meadow folded her arms. "Doesn't skill count for anything?"

Uncertainty clouded Wesley's face, but stubbornness quickly replaced it. "Well, practice doesn't hurt, of course, but God still controls where it goes."

Moose raised his eyebrows. "So God created the world and keeps the planets spinning and puts world leaders in place. Are you trying to tell me that this great God took time out of His busy schedule to make Tana's arrow hit the target?"

Wesley handed Tana another arrow. "Yes."

"Why? Is He rewarding her for some good deed she's done?"

"Maybe."

Tana shot again. The arrow fell to the bottom of a tree trunk.

Moose's eyes lit up. "And what about that one? What was that? Punishment?"

Wesley shrugged.

Tana shot three more times. Two of them actually hit the target, though they were near the edge.

"Then what about Evan Blake?" Moose said. "Did God tell that cougar to get him?"

"I don't presume to say that I understand everything God does. I just know He controls everything and nothing happens by chance." Wesley went to retrieve our arrows. Convenient timing, I thought, since Jeremy had brought the other arrows back.

Moose turned to me. "What do you think, Cody? Does God control absolutely everything we do? Does He control every shot we shoot? And if so, why didn't He protect Evan Blake?"

I was hoping he wouldn't ask me. "God is in control," I squeaked. By seventeen my voice shouldn't still be changing, but it chose this time to go out on me. "There's no such thing as luck or fate. I know that we say nothing just happens. But does God step into every situation, control every arrow we shoot? Maybe Jeremy can answer that one."

Jeremy shrugged. "Hey, I'm just a counselor, not a Bible scholar."

We called Pastor Steve over and asked him.

Pastor Steve grinned. "Actually, Cody, I think that is an excellent question for you to think about. Tell me what you come up with." And he sprinted over to help the next team.

Every eye turned to me, like since I was team captain I had perfect Bible knowledge. I had told Moose to ask the hard questions. The first hard question, however, had Jeremy stumped and Wesley, the camp theologian, running for cover. I didn't know the answer either. So were we supposed to question the hard stuff or just take everything by faith?

During free time Moose and I bought candy bars at the candy shack and wandered down to the lake to skip rocks. We sorted through rocks at the lake edge until we had a nice pile of flat ones.

The lake shone smooth as glass. Soon we were doing four skips, seven or eight, then ten. Each rock left its little trail of circles in the water. "Seven, eight, nine," I counted. "Moose, remember the little talk we had about loving God and being nice?"

"Yeah." He pitched a rock.

"Could you possibly try not to offend everyone at camp?"

"Hey, I haven't said one swear word." He hurled another rock. "Oh. You mean the tree-hugger. He's an environmentalist. He deserves everything he gets."

"OK. We're all sinners. We all deserve hell. But other than that, it's not a sin to be an environmentalist."

"Are you sure?"

"Pretty much."

"Well if it's not a sin, it ought to be."

"Look. We all have our faults." I flung my last rock. "You'll have to admit you have your share of them. Me, too. But this is a Christian camp. Most of us are Christians. We ought to be able to get along. As much as you don't like environmentalists, you don't have to bring up logging issues when Titus is around. And if you know someone is not going to like what you are going to say, maybe you should consider not saying it."

Moose grinned. "Oh, I get it. I know what's really bugging you. You're sweet on that Indian girl, and now she knows you shoot squirrels."

I could feel my face heating up. I searched the ground for more flat rocks. "I'm not sweet on anyone. I don't even want to think about girls until I'm practically through Bible college."

"You can't fool me. I see how you look at her." Moose batted his eyelashes and used his high girlie voice. "Oh Meadow, you're the fastest girls' runner in class A schools. Coach thinks you can outrun most of the runners in the AA schools. Oh Meadow, you're so beautiful."

"I never said she was beautiful. Not that she's not. She's got the kind of beauty an antelope has. But at least Meadow tries to make peace instead of disturbing it. You ought to try it sometime!"

A few ducks flew overhead, quacking their disapproval of the rocks we were throwing.

Moose leaned against a pine tree. He kicked a little pattern in the dirt. He was thinking, calculating. "So. You're gonna be my friend. You're gonna help me through camp. Until I embarrass you in front of some pretty little girl. Then you have to choose, don't you? Who is it going to be? Me or *the fastest runner in camp*? Hey, I can always go home. I never wanted to come to camp in the first place."

Moose was baiting me. I thought about everything Moose had said about his family. His dad had left them when he was a baby. His mom spent her time trying to impress various boyfriends until she married his stepdad. His stepdad saw him as more of an employee at the logging site than a son. His school buddies had dropped him as soon as he stopped drinking. So how long would our friendship last? I wasn't about to give up yet, but friendship went both ways. If I was going to help him grow as a Christian, he was going to have to flex some muscle too.

I fingered a smooth rock and pitched it sideways. It skimmed the top of the water like a motorboat leaving a line of ripples in the water. The skips were so close together you couldn't even count them. "If you think you're going to trick me into losing our deal, you can forget it." I said. "But you could try to be nice."

"I try. These people are just extra sensitive."

I scowled at him.

"OK. I'll try harder. Or you can just send me home on the second day of camp so you can impress Meadow Red Owl."

"Don't push your luck."

"Luck? I thought there was no such thing as luck. Don't you mean, don't push God's *blessing*?"

I glared at him. Moose caught my look. The lunch bell rang, and he headed away from the lake. Perhaps there was still hope. Moose had finally figured out when to shut up.

5

"Cheetah, I know snail doesn't move very fast, but you still have to keep your place in line."

"Elephant, look out for ladybug. If you don't watch your step, you'll have generations of environmentalists blaming you for the extinction of a species."

"Snake, do you mind not smiling? Your fangs are making the other animals nervous."

"Skunk, mind your manners. The smell is bad enough in here without you making a contribution."

I could just imagine Noah trying to get all the animals settled on the ark. God had made me captain of a team of people as different as some of Noah's animals. Somehow we had to work together and get along.

Maybe some of the animals on the ark hibernated once they got settled. Maybe God gave Noah some miracles to make their year on the ark work. Camp was only a week long, but I could use a miracle too.

"One spoon or two on your nachos?"

I shook myself out of my daydream. "Pardon me?"

"Do you want one spoonful or two of the meat sauce?"

"Two."

I reached for my plate and added grated cheese and sour cream. Then I searched the room for a table. Luke had a place at his table. Perfect timing.

I plunked my plate down across from his and sat on the bench. "Hey, Luke, looks like the Coyotes were having a little trouble with your bow and arrows this morning."

Luke shrugged. "Archery's not our strongest skill."

"I figured that out when I saw how many arrows hit the ground." I scooped up a messy bite. Mmmm. Mrs. Johnson always seasoned the meat sauce just the way I liked it—hot, but not too hot. "You may have been first place last night, but I'd say we came out on top with Esau's Quest."

"You have an unfair advantage. You have Meadow on your team."

"Why is that unfair?"

He glanced over at Meadow sitting at the end of our table. "Because she's, you know, Indian."

Meadow's back went straight. She eyed Luke. "What's unfair about that?"

He met her gaze. "Well, your people are always good with bows and arrows, good at boating, fast runners, stuff like that."

She folded her arms. "Right, cowboy, get off our land."

"I'm not a cowboy."

"I thought all white men were cowboys. You come and take our land, kill our buffalo, demean our culture, and force civilization upon us."

"Hey, I never killed any buffalo."

"And I don't run fast because I'm Native American. I run fast because I run a lot. Plus, God gave me natural athletic ability."

"Then why do all the fastest runners always come from Browning?"

Meadow smiled, "Because some of us enjoy exercise. Fat and lazy Native Americans don't run any faster than fat and lazy whites. I'm half Indian, about a quarter Irish, and a quarter English. The Indian half of me doesn't run any faster than the white half. I like running, so I run. If you're so worried about losing, try running more and quit blaming your bloodline."

Luke grinned at me. "Ooh, Cody. Looks like you have some feisty Grizzlies on your team."

I grinned back. "You bet we do. Get ready to lose."

43

"You say I'm feisty. Why? Just because I want people to see me for who I am?" Meadow pointed her fork at us. "You take one look at me and think you know me. I like tacos and fantasy books and science fiction. I raise tropical fish, and I surf the internet for drawings by Escher. Can you tell that by looking?"

I crunched a nacho loudly just to be cocky. "Forget about Luke. He's just worried because us Grizzlies are going to cream his Coyotes."

Luke crunched a nacho back at me. "You talk brave, but you forget us Coyotes have something you Grizzlies don't."

"What's that?"

Luke's grin widened, "Coyotes have me for a captain."

"Well, that will come in real handy, Luke, because I happen to know you like peanut butter sandwiches."

"No peanut butter for me this year. I'm waiting for my huckleberry pie. Which reminds me—time for dessert. Think I'll go get a brownie."

Luke joined the line for brownies.

Meadow scooted over on the bench until she faced me. The fire in her eyes had settled to a slow simmer. "Why am I feisty just because I want to be treated like everyone else? No one expects Tana to run fast or shoot accurately. When I do well, I'm practically accused of cheating."

"Never mind Luke. He's over-competitive."

"And you're not?"

"Not usually. Just with Luke. Eight years ago we started camp together and somehow we started competing. It became camp tradition. Now it's our last year so . . ."

"You've got to win."

"Actually, Luke is the one who has to win. I don't care that much, but it's hard to stop once you get started. It's all supposed to be about me and Luke, but I guess our teammates sometimes get caught in the middle. Sorry about that."

Her eyes searched mine. "So do you think I'm feisty?"

"This morning you were an incredible peacemaker. If there's one thing we need this year, that's it."

44

Meadow forked a nacho around her plate, making little patterns in the meat sauce. "Cody, did you ever have to stick up for something you believed in at school?"

"All the time. I try not to flaunt my values and go around telling people they're wrong if they're not like me. But you know how it is. People want you to drink or party. Guys ask you to lie for them. They want you to look at dirty pictures. Maybe girls don't do that so much."

"Girls have other problems."

"Then there's the evolution debate. I had to write a paper on origins and give a full view of evolution. After that I gave my view. Mr. Donnelly was skeptical."

"Yeah. Well, I believe God gave animals to man to use responsibly. I eat meat. I have an antelope hide on my bedroom floor. I shot the antelope myself. It was a clean shot through the heart. He died quickly. We ate the meat and wasted as little of the animal as possible."

"I don't have a problem with that."

"The issue of reintroducing wolves to Montana is a little more complicated. I can see good on both sides of the issue. I feel sorry for Titus. His dad works for the EPA. Being an environmentalist in Montana isn't any easier than being Indian."

"Yep. It's the same old battle. Environment versus jobs. It's hard to keep it in balance sometimes."

"My pastor's wife told me that Christians aren't supposed to worship nature, but they are supposed to use it responsibly. She respects the Indian culture for the way they treat animals. I don't see how anyone can take an animal's life for nothing more than target practice."

"You're right. We never should have shot the squirrels."

Meadow squinted at me. "Why? Because you think it's wrong or because it doesn't sound good."

My mouth fell open but the words came out sideways. "I . . . uh . . . well, at the time . . . but, you know what it's like when . . . no, guess you wouldn't. Moose is actually . . . when guys get together, they just . . . I just . . . it's just something I never thought about."

"Look. I don't expect you to say you're sorry if you're not. I'm just saying I don't feel right about shooting animals for sport, and if the subject keeps coming up, you can't expect me to say nothing."

"You're exactly right. I don't know what we were thinking. Shooting for sport is stupid and wrong."

"You're sure about that?"

Actually I had never thought about it before this morning. I hadn't given it much thought since. Now I longed to say the right thing, but I was pretty sure this wasn't it.

Meadow stood up to head for the dessert line. "I don't expect you to be perfect, Cody, but at least be real."

6

"Be real." Wesley had a tendency to be hypocritical, but me? I worked hard at being real. I must not have expressed myself clearly. I spoke without thinking. I didn't mean it the way it sounded. Something.

But I had no time to think about it. Pastor Steve got up to explain the next event. "At the end of day one the Coyotes were in the lead. Some of you didn't do too well at Esau's Quest, but don't be discouraged. The secret of Eureka is what?"

No one knew.

"Teamwork. The more every member of your team participates, the better chance you will have. Every day we will be awarding five hundred points to the team that shows the best teamwork."

Pastor Steve went on to explain the next part of Eureka. This part of the contest would last throughout the week.

For Montana Bible Treasures Pastor Steve gave us a list of Bible plants and animals which were also found in Montana. We would get fifty points for each picture of the plant or animal. If we brought back a sample of the plant or animal, we earned fifty extra points. Each team had its own camera. Pastor Steve had asked Titus to bring his camera for our team.

For Montana Bible Map Pastor Steve gave each team a detailed map of Montana. We had to circle names of Bible animals and objects on the map. We also had ten Bible questions whose answers came from the Montana map.

Pastor Steve gave us the rest of the week to work on those projects, but only Tuesday afternoon to find an illustration from Scripture. We had to bring an object of nature back to the dining hall and tell how it showed a Bible truth. It could not be one of the objects on the Montana Bible Treasures list.

We could use the whole afternoon to work on all this, and we could go anywhere on the campgrounds, on the lake shore, or along the road in front of camp.

I asked our team members to gather in ten minutes, then got the materials from Pastor Steve.

Moose looked at the map and lists. "Oh, boy, oh, boy! A treasure hunt! Just like we used to do in grade school!"

I eyed Moose. "Let me tell you something I learned in youth group. If I think a game sounds really lame, and I play the lame game in a lame way it ends up being, surprise, surprise, lame. But if I think a game is lame but I think, 'Hey, why not?' and I really put some energy into it, lots of time that lame game ends up being fun."

"So we get to go all over camp and look for . . ." He glanced at the list. "a lily, a bitterroot flower, a rose, a thistle . . ."

"Look. This morning you thought it would be a big laugh to put salt in a sugar bowl. The rest of the camp didn't get the joke. But your good friend Cody helped you work off the punishment for your crime. You said then that you owed me one. Well, it's time to pay up. Besides, we made a deal. You were supposed to give camp a good honest try. Playing the games with a little enthusiasm is part of that. The games are only going to be fun if you make them fun."

"Hmmm."

I ignored Moose and skimmed over the stuff Pastor Steve had given us. Soon the team was back at the dining hall. Titus brought his camera. Tana was carrying a purple backpack.

"OK," I said. "We have questions to answer, stuff to find on the map, and stuff to look for. How should we do this?"

Moose spoke up. "I think we ought to divide up and go in different directions so we can find more stuff."

I could imagine him finding a comfy spot on his bunk. I should have known better than to ask the question if I knew I wouldn't like the answer. "We've got to stick together. Pastor Steve says teamwork is the most important thing. Plus we've only got one camera, one map, and one list. Titus can take the pictures since it's his camera. Wesley, you take charge of the Bible questions. We'll give Moose the map."

"I'll be secretary," Tana said. "I can keep everything organized in my backpack."

"Great. Let's start with the Bible questions. I think we can answer some of them right away and cross them off our list."

Wesley picked up the list and started reading it aloud. "Number one. Jesus taught a parable about a wide road and a narrow road. What canyon in Montana does this story remind us of?"

Titus said, "Hellgate Canyon. Some kids in our church in Missoula go to Hellgate High School named after that canyon."

Wesley wrote that down. "Number two. Jesus told about a house built on the sand. What Montana city is this like?"

"Let's see. Helena, Billings, Missoula . . ." I ticked off the cities on my fingers. "Kalispell, Great Falls. Ha! The house on the sand fell down. Great Falls is it."

No one seemed to know the answers for three and four. Five was a town with the name of Joseph's prisoner friend. I thought of Baker, in the southeast corner.

"Number six. When Jesus died on the cross He told one of the thieves he would be with Him soon. What Montana town is named after that place?"

Tana, Meadow, and I shouted, "Paradise."

"Number seven. Jesus said He was the Good _____. What Montana town is this like? Is there a town called Shepherd?"

"Yeah," Tana said. "I think it's near Billings."

"Number eight. Our God is made up of the Father, Son, and Holy Spirit. What Montana mountain is this like? Must be something about the Trinity."

"Trinity Mountain," Moose shouted. "It's in the Bob. Well, it's either in the Bob Marshall Wilderness or the Great Bear. My uncle calls that area the Bob."

I gave Moose a thumbs-up sign.

Wesley wrote it down. "Trinity Mountain. I thought it would be something about the Trinity."

"It's not far from Hungry Horse Reservoir," Moose added.

"Number nine," Wesley read. "Jesus' mother is like what town?"

"We used to go hunting near Trinity Mountain," Moose went on. "Did anyone else know the answer to that question?"

Silence.

"Woo hoo! I knew the answer to that Bible question and no one else did."

"So," Wesley said. "What town is like Jesus' mother?"

"Well, isn't anyone going to tell me, *Woo hoo*?" Moose asked. "I've only been saved four and a half months. I don't know many Bible answers."

Titus didn't even look up. "Woo hoo," he said evenly.

Meadow met Moose's eyes. She smiled. "That was a good answer, Moose. I've lived all my life in Montana, and I didn't know there was a Trinity Mountain. We might never have gotten that question without you."

Moose grinned.

"So-o-o-o," Wesley said. "Jesus' mother was Mary. Does anyone know a town by that name."

No guesses.

Meadow looked at Moose. "Maybe Moose knows."

Moose shook his head. "Nah. Used all my biblical energy on the last answer."

"Guess we'll have to hunt for that one too. One more. What Montana town is like Galatians 6:10."

I found a Bible on a nearby table. " 'As we have therefore opportunity, let us do good unto all men.' Opportunity. It's by Butte on the interstate."

Wesley glanced down the list of questions. "We can check the map later for the other stuff.

Wesley handed the questions to secretary Tana. She started reading the list for Montana Bible Treasures. "Lily, bitterroot flower . . . Did they have our state flower in Israel?"

"Look in the parentheses." I said. "*Root of bitterness.* I think it's kind of a joke."

"Right. Rose, thistle, thorns, four kinds of trees. Here's some animals. Ant, bee, fly, grasshopper."

"There are dead flies in our dorm," Titus said. "I'll get a jar from the kitchen to catch a grasshopper."

"Several birds. Here's some harder ones. Bat, bear, deer, fox, weasel, wolf. Think we could bring Titus's shirt in?"

I shook my head. "Nope. Think they want the real thing. Meadow's a Red Owl too, but I don't think she'd pass for our owl. Too bad."

Most of us had ideas about where to find things. In about fifteen minutes we set our pile on the candy shack table. We had collected the ant, fly, grasshopper, branches from a fir and pine tree, and the picture of a dog. Titus snapped pictures of the samples. Tana organized them in a make-up case in her backpack. It wasn't a bad start, but the rest wouldn't be as easy.

All around us campers from other teams were darting here and there. Maybe we could get some clues by watching them. The Coyotes strolled out of a heavily wooded area near the back of the camp.

"Hey, Grizzlies, what's wrong? Looks like you're still empty-handed," Luke called out.

"Our secretary has everything filed and organized," I said. "Do you think we're going to share our secrets with you?"

We waited until the Coyotes walked out of sight, then we entered the woods in the same direction they had left.

"Look! A ladybug." Tana said.

"There's no ladybug on the list."

"I know, but I like ladybugs. They're so sweet."

"Is this an elm tree?"

"No."

"Then what is it?"

"I don't know, but it's not an elm tree."

51

"A snake!" Moose had our undivided attention.

Five voices sounded as one. "Where?"

"Right by Wesley's foot."

Wesley jumped six feet away, bouncing as he went.

Moose grinned. "Well, maybe it was just a stick."

Wesley frowned at Moose. I straightened out my smile. We kept hunting but weren't coming up with much. We stumbled upon a little cave in a rocky area covered over by tree roots. We leaned over and tried to see to the back of it.

"It's too dark to see anything."

"Too bad we don't have a flashlight."

"Wait!" Moose said. "I think I see something."

"What?" Wesley asked.

"In the back. See those two bright spots."

"I think I see them," said Wesley.

"Me, too," said Tana. "You have to let your eyes adjust to the darkness first."

I didn't see anything, but maybe it was just me.

"Looks like eyes," Moose said.

Tana squatted down and stuck her head back into the cave. "Do you think it's a squirrel hiding?"

"Nah," Moose said. "A squirrel would be closer to the ground. It could be a cat, but no. The eyes are too far apart. It's got to be a bigger animal."

Suddenly leaves rustled. "It's moving," Moose said. "It's ready to jump. It must be a cougar!"

Wesley sprang to his feet and raced out of the wooded area. Four of us weren't far behind him. Then Moose sauntered out, rustling leaves in his hands.

"You're right, Cody," Moose said. "Treasure hunts are fun."

Tana took off one sandal and whacked Moose on the arm with it. Wesley scowled at him. I grinned.

Meadow leaned over to me. "Guess he got us that time, didn't he?"

We ambled over to the chapel and out to the road. Teams spread out in every direction scanning the ground, searching high and low.

"There's got to be an easier way to do this than running all around," Moose said.

Wesley frowned at Moose. "It's a treasure hunt. You're supposed to run around and look everywhere."

"Let's walk down the road," Titus said. "I think one of the neighbors keeps a pet lamb in the field."

"Look!" Tana pointed down the road. "A pink rose! Just what we need!"

I shook my head. "I don't think Pastor Steve meant for us to find our treasures in other people's yards."

"He said we could get them anywhere along this road. Too bad we can't pick it." We reached the fence, and Tana leaned over it and smelled the rose.

Meadow said, "We could pick it if we had permission."

"Permission from old Mrs. Grumball?" I said. "She is the grouchiest neighbor in the whole area. Every year she calls up the camp and complains about the noise. Every year the pastors warn us to be careful not to irritate Mrs. Grumball. We have to guard our testimony. If it was the Hardings across the road, maybe, but not Mrs. Grumball."

Tana gazed longingly at the rose. "Well, Titus, take a picture of it anyway. Be sure to get the thorn in the picture."

Titus rested his elbows on the fence and clicked.

"Too bad it's on someone else's property," Meadow said. "It's got a thorn on the stem, so we could get the rose and the thorn at the same time."

I leaned against the wooden fence. "We won't find another rose, that's for sure. There are no wild roses around here. We'd probably be the only team to turn in a rose. Where does the Bible talk about roses anyway?"

"I don't know," Wesley said, "but Jesus is the Rose of Sharon."

"What does that mean?" Moose asked.

Wesley shrugged.

Tana reached out to touch the soft petals. "Don't you just want to pick it?"

"If only it wasn't grouchy Mrs. Grumball, maybe we could," I said.

Moose grinned. "The trouble with you guys is you have no imagination. You just have to picture Mrs. Grumball as the grouchy old school teacher who wants to flunk you. Wesley and I will go talk to her."

"What?" said Wesley.

"This is teamwork, remember? We're supposed to work together. So let's go talk her into letting us pick the rose. Pay attention. You might learn something." Moose started down the driveway.

Wesley trailed behind. "Maybe we could give her a tract. If we show her we care about her eternal welfare, maybe that will help."

"She doesn't want a tract. She doesn't even like living next to a Christian camp. Why would she want Christian literature?"

"You never know until you try."

"Nah. Let's make her like us first. Maybe you can give her the tract later."

Moose walked up to the door and rang the doorbell.

After several minutes Mrs. Grumball eased the door open. "What do you want?" she snapped.

Moose took off his cowboy hat and smiled. "Hello, Mrs. Grumball. We're your neighbors. You know. Moose Peak Bible Camp. I suppose you get tired of living next to a camp because, hey, kids are noisy. All the same, you could do worse. Since it's a Bible camp, they don't allow drinking and drugs and stuff. It must be refreshing to look out your window and see young people playing and never have to worry about drunk drivers and graffiti and stuff."

She put her hands on her hips. "Is there a point to this?"

"Yes, there is. Our team was just walking by and admiring that beautiful pink rose by the fence. You have lots of buds, but only one open rose."

54

She peeked around the door to see the six of us straggled down the driveway. "And the point is?"

"Well, the point is that we were just looking for a rose for a treasure hunt, and yours seems to be the only one in the area. Of course, my team members figured that you wouldn't want to give up such a nice rose, and they didn't want to even ask."

"Smart team members."

"But I just got to noticing that your car has gotten a bit dusty on these dirt roads, and maybe you'd be glad to have a free car wash. After all, you have lived next to the camp all these years. How many years has it been?"

"Nine."

"Nine years, and what good has it done you? See, I haven't been a Christian very long, but my friend tells me that there are two main rules for Christians. Number one, love God. Number two, be nice. Now Wesley here," Moose grabbed Wesley's arm and pulled him closer. "Wesley just thinks we should give you a tract. You know, a piece of paper that tells you how to get to heaven. But I said to myself, 'No. That Mrs. Grumball is practical. She'd rather have her car washed. Besides she probably doesn't trust people giving out religious literature. But if we wash her car, and do a good job of it, and don't mess up her driveway, she might just think about giving us that rose.' "

She raised one eyebrow. Cautious, but interested. "I don't trust just anyone with my car."

"I'm sure you don't. But we're your neighbors. You've lived here nine years. Sometimes there are forty or fifty kids over there. You might not like the noise, but think about it. Have you ever had to call the cops for drugs or drunken and disorderly behavior, or anything really serious?"

"Well, no."

"Ah. There you go. Now we can just apologize for wasting your time and leave, but then your car would still be dusty. It's up to you. What do you think?"

She sighed. "Oh, all right. The hose is in the front yard. There's a bucket in the garage. I'll bring you some rags and soap. Just make sure you don't step on any of my flowers."

Five minutes later the six of us were washing Mrs. Grumball's car. Moose made sure we did it right. Every few minutes the drapes on the house window parted, then came together again. We scrubbed and rinsed and dried.

Moose and I polished the front bumper. "I don't get it," I said.

"What?"

"Talk about hidden talents. Why can't you do this at camp or church?"

"I can wash cars anywhere."

"Not that. I'm talking about what you did with Mrs. Grumball. You know. Turning on the charm. Talking nice."

Moose scraped a bug off the headlight with his thumbnail. "It helps if you're in trouble or you want something really bad. Anyway, you said to play with enthusiasm. What are you complaining about?"

"Who's complaining? You can try it again sometime and I won't fuss."

Moose checked the car over to make sure we hadn't missed a spot. Titus coiled up the hose. Meadow wrung out the rags and hung them on the bucket. Tana smoothed the gravel around the flower gardens. Then Moose rang the doorbell.

"Well, Mrs. Grumball. We're all done. Why don't you check your car and see if you don't think our car wash is worth one rose."

She scowled at Moose, but she slipped into some shoes and came outside. She walked around the car once and her scowl deepened. "Well. Doesn't look too bad."

Moose grinned. "So. Would you say our car wash is worth one pink rose?"

"I suppose."

I pulled the multi-tool out of my pocket and offered her the knife.

Mrs. Grumball sliced off the rose and handed the prize to Meadow.

Meadow breathed in the fragrance. "It's lovely, Mrs. Grumball. Thank you so much."

"Well, you got your rose," Mrs. Grumball grunted. "Go on."

We scurried back toward camp, but I just had to turn around for one last look.

"Look at those Coyotes running all over the place," Moose told Wesley. "In one stop we got two hundred points that none of the other teams have a chance at. Plus, when Pastor Steve finds out about our good deed, he won't be able to resist giving us the teamwork points. All we had to do was wash a car."

"We made her smile," I said.

"Who?"

"Mrs. Grumball. When I turned around I caught her smiling. No one else has ever made her smile before."

Moose punched Wesley's arm. "See, Wes? We made her smile. Do you think giving her a tract would have made her smile?"

"Maybe we could go back and give her a tract."

"No, no, no! That would ruin it. If we give her a tract now, she'll think we only washed her car to manipulate her into reading the tract. Now she thinks she got a good deal. Mrs. Grumball will remember a good deal a lot longer than a gospel tract."

"But a good deal won't help her get to heaven."

"Neither will a gospel tract if she doesn't read it."

"But the whole point of doing something nice to someone like her is so you can tell her how to get saved."

"I thought the whole point of doing something nice was being nice. You know. Love God and be nice. Huh, Cody?"

"Right. You really can't argue with that. But Mrs. Grumball still needs to be saved. Maybe we can go back in a couple of days and give her a tract."

"See?" Wesley said. "The reason Christians want to be nice to unsaved people is so that the unsaved people will listen to them and get saved."

Moose pushed his hands deep into his pockets. "So if you knew some unsaved person was going to get saved, you'd be nice to him?"

"Sure. Anything to get him saved."

"And if you knew he wasn't going to get saved, you wouldn't?"

Wesley shrugged.

"I'm already saved, so why do you even bother to talk to me? Oh. I get it. You're trying to change me. I'm your project. You're trying to get me to talk like you, and act like you, and smell like you. Then we can have this sweet little week at camp where everyone is happy."

"You don't have to be like me, but you could try being less offensive."

Moose pointed to Wesley. "And you could try to be nice to people with no strings attached. Any door-to-door salesman can be nice to people he's trying to sell to."

"Would you have washed Mrs. Grumball's car if you didn't want her rose?"

"Good grief!" I said. "Would you guys quit arguing? We got our rose with a thorn with pictures of both. We made Mrs. Grumball happy, which is no small thing. We left a good testimony. Let's see if we can find a frog or a sheep or something."

We searched all we could on the campgrounds, then visited the candy shack and divided up for free time. During supper I realized we had completely forgotten to find a nature sample which illustrated Scripture. So had three other teams.

When Pastor Steve called for illustrations the Mountain Goats shook some salt onto a table. "Christians are supposed to be the salt of the earth," Danielle said. "Salt can be used to preserve things, like pickles. Christians should kind of preserve the earth by keeping it from being as bad as it would be if we weren't here."

Easy.

The Antelopes set a rock and a can of loose dirt on the table. They reminded us that our hearts should be soft and easy to grow things in, not hard like a rock. Pretty good.

Too bad we hadn't come up with anything.

"I've got one!" yelled Moose. Everyone stared at him. What now?

He reached over and picked up Tana, sending her pink sandals flying.

"What are you doing?" she yelled.

"Samson's riddle—the one about the honey in the lion carcass."

Pastor Mac picked up his Bible and hunted a few minutes. *"Out of the eater came forth meat, and out of the strong came forth sweetness.* Judges 14." He chuckled. "Moose has got to be the strongest guy at camp. And Tana is as sweet as they come. I think the Grizzlies deserve first place for originality."

Moose plunked Tana down so fast she nearly toppled over. "Woo hoo!" he cheered.

Pastor Steve grinned. "What can I say? Five hundred points to the Grizzlies for the best illustration of Scripture!"

Our team cheered if no one else did. I leaned over to Moose. "See? I told you learning about Samson in Sunday School would come in handy some day."

Pastor Steve waited until the noise settled down. "Our neighbor, Mrs. Grumball called the camp today and told what a nice job some campers had done washing her car. From her description of them I'd say the five hundred points for today's best teamwork also goes to the Grizzlies!"

"Woo hoo!" Everyone cheered then.

Campers started clearing the tables and chatting, but I just stared at the dining room wall. The set of mascot pictures and score cards matched the ones on the chapel wall. Mountain Goats—800. Antelopes—711. Eagles—765. Bobcats—610. Coyotes—955. Coyotes were still leading most of the teams, but now they were second to us Grizzlies with 1468 points!

"Thank you, Lord." My eyes never closed, but I prayed with all my heart. "I never expected to win, just finish well. But if we could win, if You want us to win, even if we do really well, it would really encourage Moose in his Christian life. And he needs that more than anyone else here.

"One more thing, Lord, and I mean this with the utmost respect. Instead of saying *amen* this time, I just want to say, *Woo hoo*!"

7

You don't ask for a cat's permission before you have him declawed. Dr. Walters also didn't ask Moose to take off his boots.

Wednesday morning we began Paul's Body Building. The Apostle Paul said he ran and he kept his mind on the goal. He even "kicked against the pricks" before he was saved, though Pastor Steve told us we shouldn't do that. Anyway, he said Paul played spiritual soccer. We'd play the real thing.

Grizzlies and Bobcats played the first short game in the elimination round. We won the toss, and Titus kicked off. Tana gained control of the ball and dribbled it down the field. Soon a cluster of Bobcats and Grizzlies fought for the ball. Moose's boots overpowered Hannah's sports shoe.

"Ow!" Hannah yelped.

Dr. Walters, the ref, blew his whistle. "You need to take off your boots, Moose."

"But they're the only shoes I have here," Moose protested.

"Off! We're going to play a clean game of soccer so that no one will get hurt."

Moose tossed the boots past the goalposts and walked back in his socks.

Hannah threw the ball in from the touch line. A Bobcat dribbled it down the field. We fought them for it. The ball bounced back and forth between the teams until Titus found room for a good kick and sent it speeding down the field. We all sped after it. Emily stopped suddenly, and Moose ran into her.

The whistle shrieked. "Foul," called Dr. Walters. "Moose ran into Emily."

Moose shook his head. He hadn't meant to run into her, but he was trying not to challenge the ref.

"Some of you are used to sloppy soccer," Dr. Walters said, "but you might as well know I've spent a lot of time reffing soccer, and I play by the rules."

Emily kicked the ball toward the goal and missed.

Play resumed. The Grizzlies and Bobcats were fairly evenly matched, and neither team gained much advantage over the other. The Grizzlies finally scored a point. Much later the Bobcats got one. Neither team seemed able to break the tie.

Once, the ball flew into the air heading for the touch line. Moose reached out to stop it from going out of bounds.

The whistle blew. "Hands."

"I know." Moose said. "I touched it without thinking."

Ryan kicked it in, and play continued. Soon a snarl of feet fought for the ball. Suddenly the ball shot free. Moose and Ryan ran after it. Ryan faked a kick away from Moose, then kicked the other way. Moose's foot shot out, and Ryan tumbled to the ground.

Again the whistle sounded. "Foul. Moose tripped Ryan."

Moose slammed his fist into his other hand. "Buzzard!"

I felt sure Moose hadn't meant to trip Ryan. Was it my imagination, or was Dr. Walters calling fouls more closely on Moose than anyone else?

Next time Moose got the ball, he kicked it with the entire force of his two hundred pounds. It flew Lindsay's direction. Trying to gain control of the ball, she stopped it with her leg, never flinching. The ball smacked her ankle, leaving a stinging red mark. I glanced at her face. She never made a sound, but she bit her lip, and her eyes got kind of wet. Dr. Walters eyed her, but he couldn't call a foul for kicking a ball hard.

Play slowed, while campers peeked at Lindsay to see if she was all right. Suddenly the ball rocketed into the air and hit Moose on the back of his hand.

"Hands!" Dr. Walters called.

Moose stormed over to him and glared down into his eyes. "What do you mean *hands*? I didn't hit the ball. It hit me."

Dr. Walters matched his gaze. "I call them as I see them. You touched the ball with your hand."

"I didn't have much choice. The ball flew through the air right at me."

"That's my call, Moose."

Moose moved closer. His hands hung as tight fists at his side. "Well, your call is wrong. I didn't reach out for it. It just hit me."

Dr. Walters never blinked. "I'm warning you. I called a foul, and I'm going to stick with it. You'll either accept that or you're out of the game."

"So? What do I care about your stupid game?" Moose's voice rose to a dangerous level. "You've been picking on me all game. Anyone else can do the things I do and get away with it, but you're looking for ways to call fouls on me. I still say your stupid call is wrong, and you owe me an apology."

I grabbed Moose's arm. "Come on, Moose. I'll sit out with you. The game's almost over anyway."

Moose turned and stared at me. He wasn't about to budge.

I pulled my hand away and pointed with my head in an out-of-bounds direction. "Come on. We'll just sit this one out and kind of cool down before we say something we regret."

Every eye watched Moose as he considered what do to. After many long seconds he sighed, stomped to the sidelines, and fell down on the grass.

"I didn't touch the ball," Moose grizzled. "It flew through the air and hit me before I had a chance to move a muscle."

I plopped down beside him. My voice fell to a whisper. "I know. It looked like that to me too. But sometimes refs see things differently."

I was hoping Moose would match my whisper, but Moose was never good at quietness. "Yeah, they see differently. Sometimes they see wrong!"

"They make mistakes like anyone else. But a ref is a ref. He's right even when he's wrong."

Matthew got the penalty kick. He took careful aim and kicked the ball with all his might right into the goal. The game lasted five more minutes, but Matthew's kick won the game. We were eliminated in the first soccer round.

Moose yanked blades of grass from the field. "I still think Dr. Walters was just waiting for me to make mistakes. He expected me to foul. He was ready to pounce on me for every little thing."

"Pounce. Ah, yes. Remember the cougar, Moose. Satan is a roaring cougar ready to pounce on you and destroy your Christian life. Whether or not you agree with Dr. Walters, he's the ref. You're just going to have to live with his decision."

"But it's not fair."

"Life isn't always fair."

"But he made the mistake. He should apologize to me. You keep telling me I have to apologize when I offend someone. Well, Dr. Walters offended me. He should apologize. Or are pastors exempt from that sort of stuff? Christians are supposed to apologize when they hurt people, except for pastors who have immunity and can do whatever they want. Is that it?"

"No, that's not it, but I think you're too angry to make sense out of much of anything right now. Why don't you walk down by the lake and throw rocks or something and use up some of that energy you're using to feed your anger?"

"Maybe I will!"

He jumped up and sped off toward the lake.

I sighed. It wasn't easy supporting a ref's call when you didn't agree with it.

Pastor Steve had been close enough to hear the end of our conversation. As Moose left he closed the gap between us. "Going to the lake was a good idea. Moose isn't going to listen to much of anything until he cools down. When he does, I'll talk to him."

"Do you think Dr. Walters was a little rough on him?" I whispered.

He sighed. "He watched Moose pretty closely, but I guess a ref usually does watch someone more closely when he thinks he may cause trouble. Moose will get over this. He's been through plenty of hard things in his life. But before he was a Christian, when he didn't like something, he told someone off. That doesn't work here. It must be confusing for Moose."

Dr. Walters strolled over carrying Moose's boots.

Pastor Steve reached for the boots. "I'll take those to Moose. By the time he's walked to the lake in his socks, he'll be glad to see them."

"Are you going to talk to him, or shall I?" Dr. Walters asked.

"I will," said Pastor Steve. "Moose has a lot to learn, but I think he is trying."

"Yeah," I said. "He may have argued with you, but he didn't swear, and he didn't yell. That's progress."

Dr. Walters looked at me. "I know you mean well. And I know he's a new believer. But if I allow him to publicly challenge me and get by with it, I will lose the respect of the entire camp. Moose is affecting the whole atmosphere here." He looked at Pastor Steve. "You can tell him that one more offense like today, and I'll send him home."

Dr. Walters moved away, shaking his head. He thought Moose was so bad. What would he think if he knew that this week Moose had been on his best behavior?

I wandered off to the candy shack to get a cold can of pop. I had planned to find a quiet place to think, but Wesley stopped me. "Moose was out of line!"

"I know. The Christian life is so new to him."

"New Christian or not, he has no right to challenge a referee's authority. Even unbelievers know that much. Moose has been nothing but trouble. He doesn't even try to work as a team. All he does is argue."

I sipped my pop. "It takes more than one to argue."

"Ha, ha. Very funny. Someone's got to straighten Moose out. After that soccer game I'd think you could see what he's doing to our team. I could handle losing, but Moose is making our team look bad. Like challenging my dad's call. He can't do that. The ref has the final word."

"Your dad was also wrong. He said that Moose hit the ball with his hands, but I really think the ball hit Moose. Then your dad gave the Bobcats the penalty kick, which meant they won the game. I really don't think Moose meant to touch the ball. It shouldn't have been a foul."

"But it's still not right to challenge the ref. His word is the law."

"I know that. I'm not excusing Moose. But your dad had been calling him on any little infraction during the whole game, so I can see how he would be angry."

"My dad believes in going by the book."

"Yep. But I kinda think he went by the book more closely with Moose than he did anyone else."

I pictured Moose walking into shop class with a hangover. A year ago Moose and his buddies were the curse of our high school. They didn't actually beat a lot of people, but they knew how to torment everyone in their path. You had to know Moose then to understand how far he had come.

"If you knew what Moose's life was like until he was saved," I said, "maybe you would understand why I think your dad could cut him a little slack."

"You always make excuses for Moose. You act like being a new Christian gives him the right to be rude and crude."

"I just think you need to give him some time to grow."

"Did you see how hard he kicked that ball to Lindsay? I can't believe she actually stopped it with her leg. I bet she'll have a bruise tomorrow."

"It's not against the rules to kick the ball hard."

"But she's a girl. He could take it easier on her."

"So now you want to treat the girls like weaklings?"

"It wouldn't hurt to treat them like ladies. What's wrong with y'all out here in the west? You don't hold the doors for girls. You let them carry heavy things and don't offer to help. You kick balls to them as hard as you would to a guy. I don't get it. Where's your sense of chivalry?"

"Chivalry? In case you haven't noticed, Wesley, we're not in the Middle Ages anymore."

Wesley raised his chin and crossed his arms. "Well, chivalry may be dead in Montana, but it's alive and well in Sweetwater, Tennessee—especially among Christians."

Was life really so different in Tennessee? I'd always heard that Montanans might not show their feelings much, but at least we were real. I'd choose genuine niceness over false flattery and showy manners any day. We weren't rude, we were casual.

"Well, you're in Montana now," I said. "We treat girls as equals. And in Montana Christians care about new Christians. We try to be patient with them and give them a chance to grow."

"A chance to grow is one thing, but he's making our whole team look bad," Wesley complained. "I don't mind being a gracious loser, if it comes to that. I'm not overly good at soccer myself. But we ought to be Christian about the way we play. We don't need players on our team who play rough and challenge the ref. This is Bible camp after all. It's no place for bullies like Moose."

I pictured Wesley, ten years older, evangelizing the world. Rev. Wesley W. Walters would preach to thousands, and who would repent? Good people? Little old ladies? Gag.

I pointed my finger in his face. "Listen, Wesley, this Bible camp does not exist so you can show off your Bible skills. Bible camp is supposed to help people grow in their Christian lives. Moose is a new Christian, and he needs more help than anyone else here. So maybe we ought to make him camper of the year."

I lowered my finger, but my heart still pounded. "I don't care how good you look to everyone else. I don't even care about having a good time. I just want Moose to know, or at least to think, that Christians care about each other and want to help each other."

Wesley studied the ground. He kicked a couple of pine cones. "I care about people. I want to see people saved. I pass out tracts wherever I go. When was the last time you gave someone a tract?"

"I don't know. Maybe never. I guess you win the tract-passing-out contest. But friendship is what helped Moose get saved, and I'm going to keep on being his friend if it kills me."

I finished my pop, crushed the can, and shot a basket at the trash can. It missed, and I had to go pick it up.

I stared at Wesley and dared myself to finish what I had begun. "You may be absolutely terrific at passing out tracts, but your friendship skills stink!"

8

"Look at all those lovely logs just waiting to be cut," Moose said. "Some of the guys in our logging crew used to get good timber out of here until the environmentalists complained. Oh. Sorry, Titus. I shouldn't talk that way about your friends."

Titus's eyes challenged Moose's. "You're right, Moose. You should be careful what you say. But I'll overlook it this time, especially since the environmentalists are ahead. Like you said—no one's getting timber out of here these days."

Pastor Steve had dropped each team off in a different spot in the national forest area behind camp. Matt, a counselor from Missoula, was with us. We were supposed to keep close to the road, so we wouldn't get lost, and walk back to camp. We were allowed an hour and were only two minutes into it, but Moose and Titus were already fighting. At least it was friendly fighting—I hoped.

I inhaled the fresh, woodsy air. Cut or still growing, I loved the smell of pine trees. But it was time for business. "OK, Secretary Tana. What are we looking for?"

Tana scanned the list. "There are a few plants—lily, bitterroot, thistle, elm. There are a few things we can get tomorrow near camp and some birds. Here's some hard ones—bat, bear, fox, the cougar we talked about, snake, weasel, and wolf."

I scratched my head. "I don't remember any weasels in the Bible. I wonder where that comes from."

Wesley had the answer. "I think it's somewhere in Leviticus where it talks about unclean animals."

"No wonder God considered weasels to be unclean," I said. "No one likes a weasel."

Moose grinned. "What do you mean? I love defenseless animals—especially in a good gravy."

I frowned. "Weasels aren't defenseless. They kill chickens, and mice—even snakes."

"I know. I just saw that on a bumper sticker once and couldn't help myself." Moose patted Titus on the back. "Oops. Sorry, Titus. I'm talking about your friends again."

Titus pulled away from Moose. "Some comments are so stupid, if you leave them alone, they lose the argument all by themselves."

"Chicken farmers hate weasels, but God did have his reasons for creating them," Matt said. "They keep rodents under control."

"Good point." Time to change the subject. "God created all kinds of creatures and all kinds of people. Look at us. We're all different, but each of us can add something to the team—if we work together. Does anyone see anything on the list?"

"I see something pink!" Tana shouted.

We headed for a bunch of wildflowers. The closest thing to pink were some red Indian paintbrush.

Tana smelled their musty fragrance. "OK, they're not pink, but they're still nice. I've always loved paintbrush."

"Good try, Tana," I said.

We roamed through the trees, climbed some rocks, kicked some pine cones. We spotted a hawk and took its picture. We had just entered a brushy area when Wesley jerked to a stop. "Wait! I hear something."

Branches rustled. Cautious footsteps came closer.

"It's probably just one of the other teams," Titus whispered.

Moose shook his head. "No. It sounds like one animal."

"Could be a big dog." Wesley said.

"Alone in the forest? I don't think so," said Moose. "What if it's a cougar? A real one this time?"

I told them about the Taylors who live down the road from us. They had a cougar get their kittens. "When the Taylors found them, there was nothing left of the kittens but the fur."

Titus looked skeptical. "Did they see the cougar get them?"

"No, but they saw a cougar in the bushes above their house the day before. What else would have eaten the kittens and left the fur?"

Tana shuddered. "Stop! You're giving me goosebumps."

More branches rustled. The thing was coming closer.

"It can't be a cougar," Meadow said. "If it was a cougar, it wouldn't be making all that noise."

Moose grinned. "That's right. You don't usually see or hear a cougar until he attacks. That's why they call them ghost cats. Remember?"

"Sounds like it's getting closer," Wesley whispered.

"Even if it is a cougar, which it isn't, it's not going to get us," Meadow said. "Cougars prefer small animals to big humans. If we leave it alone, it will leave us alone."

All the same, our group edged away from the thick brush and angled toward the road.

I don't know about everyone else, but I was glad to see a small deer run out. Titus clicked the camera. This was ridiculous. I'd been hiking all my life in Montana and never come close enough to a dangerous animal to do any more than take a picture.

We found a tree we thought was an elm and got a picture and sample. Meadow spotted an orangewood lily. A tiny black snake slithered in front of us once, and Titus chased after it with the camera until he got a picture of its tail.

After about half an hour we sat on some big rocks. Meadow passed around a bag of chocolate chip cookies. Leaves rustled near our feet, and we all stopped chewing to search the ground.

"Maybe it's a weasel," Tana whispered.

A chipmunk darted behind a rock. Meadow tossed out bits of cookie, and we sat motionless while the chipmunk popped out and grabbed a bite.

"OK, so it's just a chipmunk. It could have been a weasel."

Moose said, "Tana, you've lived your whole life in Montana, right?"

"Yeah."

"How many weasels have you seen?"

"None. But that doesn't mean I'll never see one. My cousin shot a weasel and had it stuffed. It's standing by their fireplace. So even if this one wasn't a weasel, at least I was close."

Moose grabbed another cookie. "Unfortunately, close only counts in horseshoes. It's like hunting. Aim at an elk and whether you come close or shoot way wide, either way you're not eating elk steak for supper."

"It's like a Buddhist who thinks he can get to heaven," Wesley said.

Moose raised an eyebrow. "How is missing an elk even remotely like being a Buddhist?"

"Well, a Buddhist thinks, you know, like he can believe whatever he believes and somehow he'll get to heaven," Wesley said. "It doesn't matter what you believe as long as you are sincere. Many roads lead to heaven. Well, he can think that all he wants, but he's not going to make it there."

Moose pushed his cowboy hat back on his head. "How do you know?"

"Because Jesus is the only way to God."

"Well, I believe in Jesus, but how do I know I'm right? I mean, isn't it a little arrogant to say I'm right and the rest of the world is wrong?"

"Not when you have the truth," said Wesley. "Christians have the truth because we have the Bible. If you don't believe that, you must not be a Christian."

"Look. I know I'm a sinner. Jesus died for my sins, and I've asked Him to forgive me and all that." Moose's eyebrows met as he puzzled out the question. "But I don't understand why Christianity and God are so exclusive. It's like, believe my way or you go to hell."

Wesley folded his arms. "You shouldn't think about things like that. Satan is just trying to get you to doubt. Doubt is sin."

"So now I'm not allowed to ask questions?"

70

"Not if you're going to question God."

I held up my hand like a stop sign. "Wait a minute. I think Moose has a good question. How do we know we Christians are right and everyone else is wrong? When we say we have the only way to heaven, that's a really strong statement. We ought to have some strong evidence to back up a claim like that."

"Don't tell me you're a doubter too," Wesley accused. "I thought this was a Christian camp."

"Believe it or not," Matt said, "Bible camp is a good place to ask questions. Relax, Wesley. The Bible's not so weak that it's going to fall apart the first time we ask it a tough question. All kinds of things point to the infallibility of the Bible: historical accuracy, fulfilled prophecy, reliable witnesses to Bible accounts. Other religious books can't come close to the Bible in the evidence to its credibility."

Wesley had studied the Bible his whole life, but he probably never had his faith challenged. Writing about creation for my biology class in Columbia Falls was scary, but now I was glad I had done it.

We left the rocks and walked through some tall grass. Suddenly a grouse rocketed out of the grass next to us, flapping his wings like a small tornado. Wesley hopped backward in surprise. Tana screamed. My heart pounded like a jackhammer.

Moose laughed. "Little jumpy, aren't we?"

Titus patted his chest like a thumping heart. "For all the noise those things make, they might as well be cougars. They may not have teeth, but they could scare you to death."

"But we're not afraid to die. We're Christians," Moose taunted.

"I don't mind heaven," I said. "But I wouldn't exactly love getting ripped apart by a cougar to get there."

"Maybe Christians go to Christian heaven, and Muslims go to Muslim heaven," Moose said.

"Sure." Wesley rolled his eyes. "And dogs go to doggie heaven, and cats go to kitty heaven. That is so lame. Why are we even talking about it? Read the Bible. It will tell you there is one God and one Bible and nothing else counts."

71

"Exactly," Moose said. "Christians believe the way we do because we believe the Bible. We believe our book is right. The Muslims believe the Koran is right. How can we tell someone else that they're all wrong because they don't believe in our book? Maybe we should just worship our God in our way and let them worship their god in theirs."

Wesley stuck his hands in his pockets and refused to say any more. I looked around the circle. Everyone else looked back at me, including Matt. So what were counselors good for?

My mind went blank. "Well, I guess that's where faith comes in. If God's truth was obvious to everyone, it wouldn't take faith."

Meadow cleared her throat. "Your god is too small, Moose. I know because my god used to be too small too. My father wanted me to believe in traditional religion. My mother came from a family who claimed to be Christian. Mom and Dad wanted me to mix the two together. I prayed to the Great Spirit. I gave him gifts and asked him to make me smart and help me get a good education. I praised Mother Earth for giving us food and everything we need.

"I loved Wind." A breeze fluttered through the trees then, adding punctuation to Meadow's words. She lifted her face into it and let it toss her hair around her shoulders. "Wind was powerful enough to destroy cities or generate electrical power. Wind was everywhere, and nothing could stop it. Always I asked Wind to make me fast so that I could run like it.

"At Christmastime I thought about Jesus, Who was the Son of the Great Spirit, greatest of all spirits. My dad told me that the Great Spirit sent Jesus to communicate with man. Jesus came to share the wisdom of His Father. Jesus taught parables from experiences He had seen. Those who learned His teachings were to pass them down from one generation to the next so that all would learn the wisdom of the Great Spirit.

"I started going to a church in Browning. Most of the people there are Native American like me. I started reading my Bible and seeing what it said God was like. I learned that God is so much more than the highest in a world full of spirits. God has no beginning because He started everything. He's got to be eternal or He would never exist at all. Who would there be to create Him? Evolution talks about one thing evolving from another, but it can never answer this question. Where did the first thing come from?"

"It doesn't take logic to figure that out," Wesley muttered. "You can read it in the Bible."

Meadow never even glanced Wesley's direction. "God never learns anything, because He already knows everything. He can do anything. God is everywhere. What can that possibly mean? He is infinite. I looked that up in the dictionary, but I still can't understand a God who is infinite, endless, without limits."

"Me neither. How can anyone or anything be everywhere? I mean, I'm standing here." Moose stood stiffly in a little patch of dust. "Am I standing in God?"

I said, "Maybe God is in space, but he doesn't take up any space. Does that make any sense?"

"That's it. You can't really make sense out of God sometimes, because He is so great, so big, so strong, so wise. It's too much for us," Meadow said. "So how can you compare a God like that with a great spirit, highest among many spirits in a spirit world? With a God like ours, there's no room for other gods. I mean, He made everything and everyone. He had his very own Son killed to give us salvation. I think He has the right to say that's the only way of salvation He'll accept."

Moose started shuffling through the pine needles again. "I see what you mean. I just don't understand very much of it."

Meadow laughed. "Who does?"

I said, "I've always wondered what God was doing before He created the earth and the angels." We were walking again. Sometimes it was easier to say risky things when you didn't have to make eye contact.

"See? That's a good question," Meadow said. "We don't know the answer to it, but it gives us a tiny idea of how endless God is."

Wesley lifted his chin. "God gives us all the answers we need. If He wanted us to know the answers to questions like that, He would tell us in the Bible."

Meadow glared at Wesley. "My pastor's wife says when you stop asking questions, you stop growing. I happen to agree with her."

Wesley didn't back down, but he looked away before Meadow did.

We turned toward the road. A small animal rattled the bushes right by Wesley. He jumped—again.

Moose smirked. "Another cougar, Wesley?"

"No, it's not another cougar." Wesley's voice was high and nasal, snotty. "Even I know that much. It's not big enough to be a cougar. I'm not afraid. It just startled me. I'll show you."

Wesley charged into the bushes like a cat out of a doghouse with a pit bull inside. A little skunk stepped out of the bushes, growling and stamping its front feet.

Wesley waved his arms like a lunatic. "Shoo, skunk. Get out of here. We don't need your—"

Suddenly the skunk turned and taught Wesley a basic rule of the Montana wilderness. Never chase a skunk.

Wesley covered his face and backed away. The putrid smell followed him. We ran to get as far as we could from the most contaminated area, but the smell pursued us. It was nasty!

I wondered why the smell just got worse the farther we went. Then I turned around and found Wesley trailing close behind.

"Wesley, get away!" I yelled. "Sorry, but you stink!"

"I know. What am I supposed to do?"

Matt plugged his nose. "When we get back to camp, we'll ask the cook for tomato juice. Lots of it. Until then, walk downwind and a long ways away."

Though I tried not to, I ended up holding my nose too. "I hate to say it, but I don't think Wesley's the only one who smells bad. I think we got some of it too."

Tana shrugged out of her backpack and pulled out a bottle of perfume. Tana and Meadow both doused themselves. Tana offered it to Moose.

He shrank back in horror. "I ain't putting any of that girly perfume on."

I held out my hand for it. "It's got to be better than the skunk spray."

Titus and Matt dabbed some behind their ears. In the end even Moose put some on. But no one got close to Wesley until we reached camp.

Wesley stripped down in the shower room. Pastor Mac came with a shovel when he heard about our problem. He'd dealt with skunks before. Wesley wadded up his clothes and set them on the shovel's scoop. Pastor Mac carried them away and burned them.

Matt brought us some tomato sauce from the dining hall. Wesley worked it into his hair and used it like soap. Then he scrubbed all over with deodorant soap. Our whole team showered before supper, but no one wanted to sit at our table. Wesley had his own table in the corner of the dining hall.

We were the talk of camp that evening, and the smell of it too. But there was one bright spot to it all.

After supper Pastor Steve announced the score at the end of day three. We lost in soccer and never made it to the playoffs. We wouldn't get points for the Montana Treasures and the Montana Map until Friday evening. Coyotes got the teamwork prize because each of their team members had found a nature sample. But the five hundred bonus points for the day went for the most interesting nature sample. Nothing came close to the smell of the Grizzlies.

9

Wesley sat alone like a leper in the corner of the dining hall. He didn't need to call "Unclean!" for people to keep their distance. His odor wafted ahead of him announcing his condition. He found another corner for chapel. As soon as it was over, he shot outside, wilting the fresh air.

Moose dared to approach. "Hey, Skunk-boy. How does it feel to take a shower in tomato juice?"

"My name is not 'Skunk-boy.' It's Wesley Warren Walters. I was named after John Wesley, and I like my name just fine."

"Who's Joe Wesley?"

Wesley rolled his eyes. "*John* Wesley was a famous evangelist in the 1700s. He started a great revival. His brother Charles Wesley wrote over six thousand hymns."

"OK. You don't have to get huffy about it. How should I know who Joe Wesley is? I've only been saved a few months, and you expect me to know the whole Bible and all of church history besides?"

Moose used to have a friend he called "Dragon-breath" and another friend whose nickname I won't repeat. Wesley, however, was clearly not amused with his new name.

"Be nice to Wesley," I whispered. "He's had a rough day."

"And whose fault is that?" Moose bellowed. "Any moron knows you don't shoo a skunk. You allow him to tiptoe away quietly. Or don't they have skunks in Sweetwater, Tennessee?"

Wesley shot Moose a dirty look. "Yes, they've got skunks in Tennessee. And believe it or not, some people can even read and write. I'm not stupid. If you weren't giving me such a bad time about the cougars, I would have been thinking more clearly, and I never would have chased the skunk."

Moose coughed. "Let me get this straight. You're blaming me because you shooed a skunk away and got sprayed?"

"Well, it's a little hard to think when someone is trying to make you look like an idiot."

"I didn't have to work very hard at that job, did I? You did most of the work yourself."

"C'mon, guys. Let's call a truce and forget about it." I headed toward the dining hall, hoping they would follow.

Moose wasn't done. "Well, Wesley, look on the bright side. You may not be the most popular guy at camp, but at least you smell interesting."

"Thanks, Moose. That makes me feel so much better."

"Hey, don't worry about it, Skunk-boy. It'll wear off eventually. I'd say the smell will be completely gone on your wedding day."

Wesley took off.

"Look, Moose," I said. "I know you're only joking, but I don't think Wesley is used to a lot of teasing. Maybe you'd better take it easy. By the way, did Pastor Steve tell you that Dr. Walters is only going to give you one more chance?"

"Yeah. He said I'm supposed to try really hard not to mess up or offend anyone. Are all Christians extra-sensitive, or is it just this group?"

"Just think about what you're doing. When in doubt—don't."

Moose and I found the rest of our team in the dining hall. It wasn't hard. We could have found each other by smell alone.

To make it easy on Wesley, our team, an obnoxious blend of skunk scent and perfume, gathered in the far corner of the dining hall.

"Meadow and I heard the Coyotes making up a cheer, so we made up one of our own," Tana said. "It has sound effects and everything!"

She taught it to us, and everyone but Moose and Wesley gave it a practice run. I told them we'd save it for just the right moment.

The game Rattlesnake was like a huge three-legged race. Each team member was tied to the next member at the leg with a strip of fabric until the whole team formed one long "rattlesnake." Each team's snake had to race the width of the dining hall without touching each other except at the ankles.

Wesley stood closest to the wall. We put Moose at the other end to keep them apart and tied our legs together with cloth strips. Moose jerked his right leg which was tied to my left leg. Since all my weight was on my left leg, I fell flat.

Titus pulled us together in a huddle so the other teams couldn't hear. "It's all in the timing," he said. "We have to move the legs that are tied together at the same time. We'll count *one, two, one, two*. On *one* the first, third, and fifth in line move their left legs while the others move their right. *Two* is the other way around."

As we shuffled back into a line, other teams were falling like dominos. Titus's advice was perfect, but it wasn't so easy to carry out. We practiced leaning on one foot, stepping with the other, working out a rhythm. After several falls our wobbly snake actually made it to the other side of the dining hall. Then we had to turn around. Not easy.

"Tana, I think we need that cheer now," I said.

Tana whispered it to all of us so we'd get it right. Then, with a "one, two, three" we called out. "Owls hoot, Coyotes howl. Elk bugle, Grizzlies growl. Bobcats purr and Cougars scream. We're the best, the Grizzly team!"

By this time the Coyotes, who had been watching us and using our strategy, had made their way to our side of the dining hall. Luke cleared his throat and announced, "I think we all need to congratulate the Grizzly team. The Coyotes may have spirit, but Grizzlies have smell. I thought the Coyotes were determined to win, but even we wouldn't be picking fights with skunks for an extra five hundred points! In honor of the Grizzlies' brave determination, Sarah, here, has made up a cheer."

"Give me a P," Sarah yelled.

Coyotes echoed, "P."

"Give me a U."

"U."

"What's that smell?"

"Grizzlies. Pee-yoo! Wesley, Wesley, he's our man. If we can't smell him, nobody can."

"Cute," was what I said. What I wanted to say was, "You know, Wesley's not taking this skunk thing very well, so could you please not tease our team so much?" After all, Luke wasn't mean. He wasn't trying to make Wesley feel bad. He was merely continuing eight years of rivalry. But it was a little late to stop now.

Our team never did get turned around. We had to untie our cloth strips and walk separately back to the starting line.

Pastor Steve had gone down the line, offering suggestions to all the teams. By the time we were ready to start, each team had some sort of strategy for moving. All six teams lined up side by side in six snakes. Just as Pastor Steve put the whistle to his mouth, Tana yelled, "Wait!"

"What is it?" Pastor Steve asked.

"Meadow and I have another cheer worked out."

Meadow and Tana eyed each other and took a deep breath. "C'mon Grizzlies, grin and growl. We can make those Coyotes yowl. Watch us scratch and watch us bite. C'mon Grizzlies, fight, fight, fight!"

So much for hoping the Coyotes would go easy on us. Pastor Steve grinned and blew the whistle.

"One, two, one, two," called Titus. We began our shuffle.

The Bobcats dominoed.

Half of the Coyote team passed us while the tail of their snake did a balancing act.

We lost our rhythm and started to wobble.

"Remember, no hands!" Pastor Steve said. "You can't touch each other except at the ankles."

Three quarters of the way there Moose took a tumble and took us down with him. The Coyotes fell over the finish line without actually walking over it.

I pulled my legs together with the legs they were attached to and stood up. "Come on, team, get up. Pastor Steve may call that a win for the Coyotes, but we can still finish. No one's going to call the Grizzlies quitters!"

Moose lay back on the floor, exhausted. "Forget it. This game's too hard."

"He's right," Titus said. "Look around you. You're the only one on your feet."

The Coyotes were still down. The Eagles were grounded near the starting line. They had never gotten the hang of it. The other three teams looked too weary to go on. All of the teams had come to a stop, and no one seemed to have the energy to re-start.

I looked at Pastor Steve. Were we going on or quitting?

"Good try, everyone," Pastor Steve said. "Maybe we'll call that good enough and have some refreshments."

We worked at the knots in the cloth strips. I had tied the cloth between Moose and me a little too tight. As I struggled with the knot, I noticed Moose's wallet had fallen out of his pocket. Wesley grabbed it. I didn't think any more about it until I saw Wesley holding Moose's driver's license.

"Malcolm the third?" Wesley announced his finding in a loud voice. "*Moose* stands for *Malcolm*?"

Fire burned in Moose's eyes. He yanked his leg free, jumped up, and snatched the license and the wallet from Wesley.

"Hey, Moose," Luke called. "Is your name really Malcolm? That's hilarious!"

Little groups buzzed with excitement, and *Malcolm* stuck out of every conversation.

"Well, Malcolm," Wesley said. "Now we finally know what to call you."

"Shut up, Wesley! You can call me Moose like everyone else!"

"Really, Malcolm, why should I call you Moose when you have such a lovely name?"

Moose's eyes flashed, but for once words had failed him.

Wesley grinned. "Tell you what, Moose. If you call me Wesley, I'll call you Moose."

Moose only scowled and bolted out the door. As I watched him go I thought of all the names Moose had been called at school. I had heard people say some nasty things to Moose, but he always had a comeback—until now.

Moose and Wesley, or should I say Malcolm and Skunk-boy, slept in a quiet room that night. While they slept, their anger simmered. Breakfast passed without incident, but the anger had begun to boil.

After breakfast we played Manna in the Wilderness. The rules were simple. Two large trash cans stood at either end of the soccer field. One held water. The other held flour. Everyone was given a paper cup. At the whistle half of each team could get water in their cups and throw them on the other teams. The other half could use flour. When Pastor Steve blew the whistle again, time was up. The cleanest team won with six hundred points. The dirtiest team lost with one hundred points. Everyone else came in between.

Tana, Titus, and I waited with the group by the water can. Wesley, Moose, and Meadow stood near the flour. Pastor Steve blew the whistle. I filled my cup, ran past the attack line, and flung my whole cup of water at Ryan. He threw his water at me, and we raced back to the can. I filled my cup several times and doused several people who also had water. To be really effective, however, I needed to reach the flour side. The flour and water mix would do the most damage.

As I sped away with my water, Luke called, "Hey, Malcolm!" and dumped a cup of flour on Moose's chest.

Nathan hurled flour at Wesley's legs. "Maybe that'll kill the skunk smell," he said.

I swung around to get Ryan and splashed the whole cup of water in Meadow's face. I stopped in my tracks. "Sorry, Meadow. I didn't mean to hit you."

Luke pitched his cup at me and floured my middle.

I quit apologizing and ran for more water. Before I could empty it I saw Moose dump his flour on Wesley's head. "Oops," Moose said. "I missed."

I stumbled and spilled my water. On the next pass a flour-faced Wesley poured his cup down Moose's back. "Guess I missed too." Then two girls doused them with water to make sure the flour stuck.

With my next cup of water I caught Moose and Wesley bombing each other again.

"Hey, Grizzlies," I yelled. "Don't forget who your team members are." Danielle used my lapse in concentration to shoot flour at my shoulders. I puffed the floury mist from my face and spilled my water.

"Looks like the Grizzlies want to lose," Luke called. "Let's help them out."

Suddenly all five other teams all turned on the six of us. We could not escape the steady barrage of flour and water. We cowered together in the middle, covering our heads like victims of a flour mill explosion in the middle of a downpour. The flour and water cans emptied quickly, and Pastor Steve blew the whistle.

We grouped into teams, and the Pastors came by to study us. The first five positions would be hard to judge, but there was no contest for last place. All six Grizzlies were covered with flour from head to toe.

The pastors huddled to compare notes. Then Pastor Steve announced the results. The Mountain Goats who were only slightly dusty got six hundred points. The other teams fell in behind them at five hundred, four hundred, three hundred, and two hundred.

"As for the Grizzlies," Pastor Steve said, "our panel of judges doesn't feel they deserve one hundred points. In fact, because Eureka is all about teamwork and the Grizzlies showed an appalling lack of it by attacking each other, we are going to subtract one hundred points from their score."

Other teams buzzed with comment, but the Grizzlies slapped at their floury clothes and kept quiet.

"Hey, Captain Cody," Luke taunted. "The Coyotes want to win, but we don't expect your team to help us out. Looks like your cheerleaders need to work on Malcolm and the smelly one."

I tried to think of a comeback, but my mind went blank. Luke could tease me all he wanted if he just wouldn't give my teammates such a bad time. But what could I expect? We'd been the best of enemies for eight years. If I expected favors from Luke, I would have to be his friend.

It occurred to me that Luke would make a good friend if I hadn't gotten on his bad side from the beginning. Moose on the other hand was a very difficult friend. This week at camp would have been so much easier if Luke had been my friend and Moose had been my enemy. But I had asked God to run my life, and He seemed to think that the worst of friends should be my best friend. No one said living for the Lord would be easy.

As people wandered away, I made a useless effort to shake the flour from my shirt. Moose picked at the thick floury goo in his hair, flicking what he could on the grass.

When everyone else was out of earshot I asked Moose. "What was that all about? Did you and Wesley forget you were on the same team?"

"How could I forget a thing like that? We are forced to spend practically all day together, every day, as a team. But that doesn't mean we have to win. When else am I going to be able to absolutely cream Wesley and not get in trouble for it?" Moose grinned.

"Well, you didn't help our team any. Not only did we get absolutely no points for totally losing, Pastor Steve even deducted points because we were such a negative example of teamwork."

Moose gave up on his hair and brushed at the flour on his pants. "So? It was worth it. Wesley deserved it. He had to tell all of western Montana what my real name is."

"You called him Skunk-boy."

"Which is only appropriate after he was stupid enough to chase a skunk. But no one has ever called me Malcolm. Mom named me after her dad and granddad, but even she had enough sense not to call me that. I was Moose from the time I was born weighing over ten pounds. I registered for kindergarten as Moose Richards. All through school I guarded my name. Can you imagine what will happen at high school next year when my ex-buddies find out my name is Malcolm the third?"

I slapped my jeans. "Maybe they won't find out."

"Our whole youth group knows. Our school competes with schools that all these campers go to. You think thirty six campers will be able to resist leaking news like that?"

I wanted to say no, but I had told Moose that lying was sin.

Moose picked thick flour/water paste off his shirt. "I never should have let you talk me into coming to camp. You said people here would be nice, that Christians care about each other. You said they would understand that I'm a new Christian and expect me to make mistakes."

"Right. You've got to allow Wesley to make mistakes too."

"OK then, let me ask you something. How long has Wesley been saved?"

"Well, I heard him say once that he was saved when he was five. He's seventeen now. I guess that's twelve years."

"And he was raised in a Christian home, a preacher's home, for heaven's sake. He has gone to church all his life. He home schools using Christian books so he doesn't have to get evil teaching at public school. He probably knows more about the Bible than any other camper here, wouldn't you say?"

I blew flour off my glasses and searched for a clean spot to wipe them on. "Yep. I guess so."

"Well, you keep telling me that I need to grow in my Christian life, that I just need to keep progressing, that it'll get easier. Once I get used to 'the discipline of living the Christian life,' I'll get better at it. Right?"

"Yep."

"So tell me. What have I got to look forward to? After I've been a Christian twelve years, if I go to church every Sunday and work real hard and study my Bible, what will I be like? Wesley?"

Moose waited for an answer. He didn't get one.

"Well," he said, "if that's what the Christian life is about, you can forget it."

10

My miracle was slipping away from me. I'd made a deal with Moose, and I was going to lose. Moose wouldn't win either. Moose had conquered drinking, smoking, and swearing. He had begun to grow as a Christian. Now as he stood wavering between going on and giving up, one thing made him want to quit. That thing, that person, was Wesley.

I wanted to shake Wesley, to choke him. I wanted to scream and yell and lose my temper.

Satan was a roaring cougar ready to pounce. He wasn't just destroying Moose and Wesley. He was working on me too. I had to get a hold of myself.

I paced the soccer field waiting for everyone else to shower first. So what if the water was cold?

"Why, God? Why do You allow stuff like this to happen? I know You're in control, but I don't get it. Moose isn't the easiest guy to get along with, but he is trying. At least he was trying."

Somehow Moose and Wesley's little squabbles had turned into full scale war. And I had thought a Christian camp with Christian fellowship would be good for Moose.

"OK, God. I know that Moose has pushed Wesley. I know Wesley's not used to being teased. But Moose is right. Wesley has been saved for twelve years. He wants to be an evangelist and win people to Christ. Shouldn't he be mature enough to ignore some of Moose's comments? I don't want to be judgmental, Lord, but Wesley seems like such a hypocrite."

Why did God allow hypocrites like Wesley to live? I wondered, yet I knew at the same time. It was God's almighty patience. I needed to talk to Wesley, but before I did, I prayed that God would share some of His patience with me.

As I showered I tried to figure out what to tell Wesley. Finally I felt an uneasy peace. If I went to Wesley with the right attitude, I felt sure the Lord would help me know what to say.

As I searched the camp for Wesley, I ran into Pastor Steve. He said Wesley was out on the dock.

"When I made you captain, I didn't expect camp to become World War III," he said. "After this week maybe we'll give you a purple heart."

"Yeah. Wesley wants to be an evangelist. You'd think he'd be good with new believers. Guess he and Moose just aren't a good combination."

"Well, it was my idea to put them on the same team. I prayed about the teams when I picked them and God allowed that. I'm not sure why. When I talked to Moose the other day, I felt he listened to me and was willing to try harder not to offend people. They might have gotten along OK if it weren't for the skunk and Wesley finding out Moose's real name. That Manna game can get rough, but today it was downright vicious."

"Yep."

Pastor Steve sighed. "Well, I talked to Moose. I guess it's time I talked to Wesley. I really think he's the one with the bigger problem right now."

He turned toward the dock, but I stopped him. "Wait. I was on my way to talk to him anyway."

"I don't expect you to do that."

"Isn't that why you made me captain, so I could practice being a leader?"

He frowned. "You want to talk to Wesley?"

"Not much. But, hey, a leader's got to do the hard stuff sometimes, right? I've had to say hard stuff to Moose, and he's a new believer who gets mad easily. I ought to be able to talk to a twelve-year-old Christian who at least thinks he's trying to do what's right. Don't you think?"

"OK. Just remember the last twenty-four hours haven't been easy for Wesley either."

"I know. I promise not to choke him, even if I feel like it. I've been praying about this, but I don't mind if you pray too."

"You got it, Cody."

I found Wesley on the dock dangling his feet in the water. He had showered after the skunk, then again that morning, then after the Manna game. It must have taken him a while to get all the flour scrubbed out of his dark hair. He was starting to smell a little better.

The dock rocked back and forth as I sat beside Wesley.

Wesley didn't even glance my direction. "If you've come to make more excuses for Moose and yell at me for not treating him better, you can save your breath. Moose deserved everything he got this week—and more."

I took my shoes off, rolled up my pants, and dangled my feet besides his. "Tell me about Christmas at your house."

"Huh?"

"Christmas. Do you have family traditions and stuff?"

"Sure. Mom makes sugar cookies and us kids decorate them. We cut out snowflakes and build a snowman family on the front lawn. Our family searches the forest for the perfect Christmas tree. Each year each kid gets a new Christmas decoration for the tree. Dad takes the boys shopping, and Mom takes Susannah. You mean stuff like that?"

"Yep. And then there's church stuff, right?"

"Yeah. Mom always directs the Christmas program. Last year she didn't want me to feel silly playing a wise man, so she sewed me this costume that really looked authentic. Of course, Dad preaches his special Christmas sermons. Billy, Dwight, and I sing in the church choir. Charles will next year."

"What do you do on Christmas day?"

"Normal stuff. Before we open our presents we read the Christmas story. Dad always reminds us about the people we were named after: John, Charles, and Susannah Wesley, Billy Sunday, and Dwight Moody."

"Your mom and dad named you all after evangelists?"

"Yes. Well, Susannah was an evangelist's mother. And Charles was an evangelist's brother. Did you know he wrote more than six thousand hymns?"

"You mentioned it."

"After I preached my first sermon, Dad told me he knew what Samuel Wesley must feel like. It was the nicest thing he ever said to me."

"What's that supposed to mean?"

"Well, Samuel Wesley wasn't much of a preacher himself, but John and Charles brought revival to England and the rest of Europe and even America. I guess Samuel Wesley must have looked down from heaven after he died and been very proud of his sons . . . and his wife."

"So back to Christmas day at your house . . ."

"Mom makes homemade sweet rolls for breakfast and a big turkey dinner. Our budget is pretty tight, but Mom always manages to come up with some pretty nice presents. But as Mrs. Grumball would say, is there a point to this?"

I splashed little ripples in the water with my toe. "Moose's family spends most of Christmas vacation drunk. His mom gives him a check for Christmas so he can buy what he wants. Christ's name is only mentioned as a curse word. His parents always fight, but it gets worse during the holidays."

"And the point is . . . ?"

"We're rich, Wesley. You and I have so much. Moose may live his entire life in western Montana. When word gets around that his name is Malcolm the third, he'll never live that down."

"Come on. Malcolm isn't that bad."

"It is if he thinks it is. To Moose it's like wearing a necklace or a pink shirt. Moose has built up this macho image and guys in Hungry Horse will use his name to torment him. They're already teasing him about being religious and not drinking."

"He shouldn't have called me Skunk-boy. I say we're even."

"Wesley, look at your family life, your church life, and his. Do you really call that even? Do you really think that with all the advantages God has given you, that He expects no more from you than He does from Moose?"

Wesley sat still as a stone.

I stood up, grabbed my shoes, and staggered down the rocking wooden dock. I was no good at this sort of thing. I had so much I wanted to say to Wesley, yet all I could talk about was Christmas. Still, I had asked God to help me know what to say and that's what came out. I guessed I'd have to leave the results with Him.

Teamwork was the key to winning Eureka. But if our team had any more togetherness, it would explode. I had to figure out how we could do some of our teamwork separately.

That afternoon we had another hour to work on the Montana Treasures and the Montana Map.

I sent Moose out on the lake with a fishing pole to catch a fish.

I gave Wesley the Montana map and suggested he hunt for Bible items. Ruby River, Ruby Dam, Ruby River Reservoir, Ruby Range. Then he started all over looking for fox, sheep, wolf, and bear. Wesley was hardly an expert on the Montana map, but it kept him out of trouble.

Meanwhile Titus, Meadow, Tana, and I hiked down the road to find the chickens, a cow, a horse, and a frog.

We found the farm animals. Moose caught a fish. But I was not looking forward to supper and score time.

Thursday had not been a good day for our team. We lost one hundred points for Manna in the Wilderness. Our Montana Treasure and Montana Map points would not be added until the next day. Add to that no bonus points and our team actually went backward!

I stared at the score cards. Coyotes—2855. Bobcats—2010. Eagles—2165. Antelopes—2161. Mountain Goats—1900. And Grizzlies in last place at 1868. How could we be way ahead on Tuesday night and plummet to rock bottom by Thursday night?

Luke sauntered by. "I can hardly wait for my huckleberry pie," he whispered. "Though I'm sure the cooks will put their absolute best effort into your peanut butter and jelly sandwiches."

To Luke, Eureka was merely a continuation of friendly rivalry that began eight years ago. If only it were that simple, that all that hung in the balance was Friday night's supper.

After supper Moose wandered off into the trees. He was probably missing his cigarettes and needed to walk it off. I ambled out to the gate and sat on the fence waiting for chapel. A day and a half left of camp. If I could keep Moose and Wesley from killing each other, we might actually finish it. But I couldn't see any hope for Moose going away satisfied. I wanted to help Moose, but I was completely out of ideas. Barring a miracle, Moose might just give up church for good.

I sat for a while, then noticed Meadow running down the road toward me. She stopped by the gate. "Guess what?" she said. "I just ran with a deer."

"What do you mean?"

"Well, I decided it would be a nice time for a run. I put on my running shoes and took off down the road. Pretty soon I saw this baby fawn. He started running down the road the same way I was. I kept looking over at him, and he kept running beside me. He ran with me for about a quarter of a mile, then took off into the woods."

"Wow. I don't imagine he'll be doing that once hunting season starts."

"No. Anyway, I just felt like telling someone about it and here you were."

"Thanks. I'm glad you told me. I'd love to run with a deer sometime, only I don't really run. At least you'll have one good thing to remember about camp this year."

Meadow smiled. "It hasn't been that bad."

"It hasn't been that good either. Not for the Grizzlies. I'm sorry about that. It's not usually like this, you know. Oh, Luke and I give each other a bad time. But I've never seen fighting like this year. I guess Moose and Wesley just don't do well together."

Meadow leaned against the gate and picked three long weeds with feathery ends.

I plucked a weed too. "By the way, this morning I didn't mean that water to hit you in the face."

"I know."

She braided the weeds into a perfect ribbon, then weaved the braid into her hair. Weird, but on her it looked natural. "Cody, you're a really good friend for Moose. I know sometimes it might seem like you are getting nowhere with him, but I don't think that's true."

"I don't know about that. I've tried to talk to him about so many things, but right now I feel like I've run out of things to say."

"Then just keep on being a friend. It's tough making sense of everything when you're a new Christian. It takes time to figure stuff out. Sometimes you get it wrong, but it helps so much to have a Christian friend who doesn't give up on you when nothing else makes sense."

How did Meadow always know how to say just the right thing? I looked up to thank her, but she was gone. She left me holding a feathery weed and a deeper sense of peace. As bad as things looked right now, I thought things might turn out all right after all.

Somehow when I left the fence I couldn't throw the weed down. I cut off the end, stuck it in my Bible, and went to chapel. Wesley and Moose sat on different sides of the chapel and ignored each other. I fingered my weed and kept my peace.

In his sermon Pastor Mac talked about targets. I decided our team should have been called Targets instead of Grizzlies. Wesley was Moose's target. Then Moose became Wesley's. I was caught in the middle and got it from both sides. Our whole team became the target of the flour and water bombs.

Pastor Mac, however, talked about deciding ahead of time what you were going to do in times of temptation so you could stay on target. He talked about setting goals, targets, and working toward them, asking God to lead you. He talked about long range goals and short range goals to get to the long range ones.

My long range goal was to be a missionary. My short range goal was to make it through another day and a half of camp. Somehow I felt that a lifetime of work with unknown foreigners would have to be easier than a day and a half with Moose and Wesley.

After chapel we played a chopsticks and M&M's game. Tana, Meadow, and Titus did a pretty good job of carrying the M&M's with chopsticks from one bowl to the other. Moose and Wesley stood watching with arms folded, scowling at each other. When their turns came, they obviously didn't care and dropped most of their M&M's. When my turn came, the rest of the teams had finished. I could have just skipped it, but all week long I'd been telling my team, "We won't always win, but we can finish with our heads held high."

Slowly, carefully, I lifted the last M&M and dropped it into the bowl, pretending not to be embarrassed.

Then I glanced at Moose. He was grinning. Why? I didn't trust grins I didn't understand, and this grin looked particularly suspicious.

Friendly chatter from other teams filled the quiet spaces from ours. None of the Grizzlies had much to say. We wandered away to our dorm rooms and undressed quietly. With Wesley and Moose not talking, our room quieted down before any of the others. Soon I was fast asleep.

About two thirty I awoke with a start. I lay silently, listening. Nathan snored. Ryan rolled over. I got out of my sleeping bag and stood up. Moose's bunk was empty. He'd downed a can of coke before bedtime. I decided to check the little boys' room.

I slipped on my flip-flops and shuffled down the hall. No one was in the restroom. I checked in the shower room. No one.

I stepped outside and scanned the semidarkness. Pine needles scrunched. I walked around the dorm to find a doe nibbling some grass. She raised her head, met my stare, continued eating. Thick clouds covered the moon and stars, and a cool wind tugged at my pajama legs making me shiver.

Back inside I checked the dorm shower room and the restroom again. Nothing. I listened at the door to each room but heard only the normal sleeping noises. Weird.

I opened the door to our room and squinted into the darkness. Moose was back in bed. He faced the wall. He wasn't snoring, but what did that mean? Had I only dreamed his bunk was empty? Maybe he had just been scrunched down in his sleeping bag.

I slipped back into my sleeping bag, but sleep didn't come right away. The inner peace I had felt with Meadow had completely vanished.

11

I was brushing my teeth, trying to wake my mouth up when Wesley stumbled into the bathroom. I glanced over at him, then spit toothpaste into the sink. Was I still half-asleep or did Wesley look different this morning? I looked again. Oh no. What now?

Ryan noticed, too. "Hey, Wes. Nice hair."

"I know," Wesley mumbled. "My hair always sticks up in the morning."

Wesley picked up a wet washcloth with his thumb and forefinger and let it drop to the floor. He set his own towel and shampoo in its place. He turned the water on, then glanced into the mirror. Suddenly his eyes grew wide, and his mouth dropped open.

"Who dyed my hair?" he demanded. "It's blond right down the middle! I look like a . . . like a skunk!" He glared at me. "It was Moose, wasn't it? It's just the kind of thing he would do."

"Why accuse him?" I asked. "It could have been anyone."

"It had to be Moose. He's been calling me Skunk-boy ever since I ran into that skunk. What am I going to do? I can't go anywhere looking like this! That Moose has gone too far. This stuff had better wash out or I'm going to—"

Wesley stomped over to the shower. One sock flew over the shower door, and a T-shirt fell askew over the top.

A few more guys stumbled sleepily into the room, but my eyes stayed glued to the shower door. Steam and vigorous scrubbing noises drifted into the room. Then out stomped Wesley holding a towel around his middle. He checked the mirror. "The streak is still there! What did he do, bleach it? It'll never wash out. How could he? That Moose Richards is going to pay for this."

Just then Moose strolled in. He grinned. "Hey, Skunk-boy, looks like your true character is finally coming out."

"You did this, didn't you?"

"Now what would make you think I did it?"

"No one else would do such a horrendous thing."

"Who says it's horrendous? It gives you a little style. And it makes you not look so serious. That has to be good."

"You're in big trouble, Moose Richards!"

"Why? I never said I did it. I just said it improves your looks."

"It makes me look like a . . . like a . . . like an unbeliever!"

"Ooooo." Moose's tone mocked Wesley's words. "An unbeliever! Is that the worst thing you can come up with? Until a few months ago I was an unbeliever."

Wesley growled at Moose. Finally Wesley stomped back into the shower. He dried and dressed noisily and stomped from the room, dropping one sock on the way. Every eye followed him out the door. As the door slammed, the air exploded with whispers and laughter.

"Come on, Moose," I said. "We have to talk."

I led Moose down the hall to a large cleaning closet. We both went inside. I closed the door and pulled the light string. "Did you bleach Wesley's hair?"

Moose shrugged. "Sure. Why not? He deserved it."

"What's Wesley going to have to do to get rid of the skunk look?"

Moose balanced a feather duster on one finger. "Relax. It will grow out. My mom has to redo her roots every six weeks."

"You used your mom's hair color—which you just happened to have along."

"You said to come prepared. What's the big deal anyway? Other people play pranks and people laugh. I play one, and Wesley gets all mad about it. Where's his sense of humor?"

I fanned my face. Some cleaner with ammonia was making it hard to breathe. "Pranks are innocent when they don't make people feel bad. You made Wesley feel stupid."

"So? What do you think I feel like when everyone calls me Malcolm. And when my teammate rolls the kayak. And when he announces to the whole camp that I ruined the coffeecake. And then there's the Bible drill. Wesley's always the first one up. Then he accuses me of cheating because I'm looking up the books in the index. How am I supposed to know where Second Romans is?"

"There's only one Romans."

"See? Wesley knows every answer to the Bible quiz. I don't know any. He treats me like he's a Bible college professor and I'm a spiritual moron. Think of how that makes me feel."

"Wesley has been in church all his life. His family studies the Bible at home. He may know his Bible, but you are better at sports."

"Tana tried to tell me the same thing. 'Everyone adds something to the team,' she said. 'Some people are better at Bible stuff, and others are better at sports or target practice.' I listened at first, but I'm not buying that any more. Here at camp, if you're good at sports, fine, and if you're not, that's OK too. But knowing the Bible is all anyone cares about. If you know the Bible, everyone thinks you're some kind of saint. Nothing else counts."

I opened my mouth to reply, but what could I say? Moose was right.

Moose dusted the light bulb with the duster. "Remember when you talked me into coming to camp? You said that it would be this wonderful Christian atmosphere where everyone would care about me. They would understand that I was a new Christian and expect me to make mistakes. 'Love God and be nice,' you said. As long as I did that, I would be all right."

"I kind of think making Wesley look like a skunk would violate that *be nice* rule."

"Other people pulled pranks, and I pulled pranks. Their pranks were funny, but no one laughed at mine. So where's that love and forgiveness you told me so much about?"

I sighed. "Well, Moose, Dr. Walters was only giving you one more chance. I don't think he's going to feel very loving and forgiving when he sees the way you used his son for your nifty little fashion statement."

Moose shrugged. "Let him send me home. I don't care. And if Wesley wants to be a preacher some day, well, I could preach him a sermon. I'd say. 'Wesley, love God and be nice.' " Moose shook his finger at invisible Wesley. "That skinny flatlander from Sweetwater, Tennessee may have been reading his Bible since he was five. He may be the fastest Bible drill champion in the west. And he may have half the New Testament memorized. But what's the point of knowing your Bible and being a Christian if you're not nice?"

I opened my mouth to answer, but my brain was filled with blanks. What could you say to a question like that?

I had been so worried about what all these nice Christians would think of Moose. Meanwhile Moose, like a hunter tracking deer, had spotted every bad attitude and bit of hypocrisy in these "nice Christians." What was it about Moose that brought out the worst in everyone? And what could I do to protect Moose and his clumsy, newborn faith? I tried to think of one reason why Dr. Walters would allow Moose to finish the week of camp, but nothing came to mind.

I dreaded breakfast and would have skipped it entirely, but I knew we would have to face Dr. Walters sometime. Sure enough, he was standing tall, like a soldier, beside the door to the dining hall. The second we got close he motioned us to one side.

"Moose, are you responsible for the streak in my son's hair?"

Moose shrugged. "I can't take all the credit. I got a little help from my mom's hair color stuff."

"So did you act alone on this little prank, or did you have help?"

Moose looked at me, then back at Dr. Walters. "If you mean, did Cody have anything to do with it, the answer is no."

"Did anyone else have anything to do with it?"

"Nah." Moose grinned. "Except for Wesley. I couldn't have done it without him."

Dr. Walters shook his head. "Well, Moose, you ruined the camp coffeecake. You publicly challenged my authority as the soccer referee. Pastor Steve warned you about your behavior. Now this. I can't continue to overlook your offenses."

"Hey. It was a joke. He got sprayed by a skunk. The whole camp thought that was hilarious. We won the prize for the most interesting nature sample for heaven's sake. It's just hair color. He can dye it back when he gets home, or he can cut his hair really short. What's the big deal?"

"The big deal is that you are hurting other people, and you don't seem to be the least bit sorry."

"Wesley deserved what he got. If you don't like my behavior, send me home. I don't care."

Dr. Walters closed his eyes for a second and took a deep breath. "With an attitude like that, I'm afraid I'm going to have to. As soon as breakfast is over you can go to the dorm and pack your bags."

"No! You can't do this!" The words escaped from my mouth before I could pull them back.

Dr. Walters raised his brows at me

"Please, Dr. Walters. Give Moose one more chance!"

"I've given Moose all the chances he's going to get. Now he's got to bear the consequences for his actions."

I bit my lip. "If he goes, I'm going too."

"That's up to you, but don't rush into something you'll regret later."

Anger, hurt, confusion, frustration, worry all threatened to explode.

"Come on, Moose," I said. "Let's get out of here."

12

I had half expected Dr. Walters to send Moose home, but now that he had, I felt flattened. I had lost. Now Moose would leave camp and never come to church again. How could Dr. Walters do this?

When we came to camp, my worst fear was that Moose would hate camp and want to leave. Moose had played games he thought were lame. He worked with teammates he disagreed with. His soccer was over-refereed. His pranks were under appreciated. Wesley had shared his most guarded secret with everyone at camp. And while Dr. Walters thought Moose was stirring up trouble, Moose was actually showing a lot of self-restraint. Now that Moose actually wanted to stay, Dr. Walters was sending him home.

Didn't he realize Moose's spiritual life was at stake here? Why couldn't he just let Moose stay one more day and finish out the week? If Pastor Mac was camp dean, he wouldn't be sending him home. I felt sure about that. There had to be something I could do to reverse Dr. Walter's decision.

Moose took off, and I paced the campground. Finally I decided to talk to Pastor Mac. Hunting for him, I ran into Luke.

"Hey, Cody. I know the Grizzlies are losing, but that's no reason to quit and go home early."

"It's not about you and me. Consider yourself the champion if that helps. Have you seen Pastor Mac?"

"Not since breakfast. Are you really leaving camp?"

"Looks like it. I don't want to. Believe me. But I guess Moose just messed up one too many times. Dr. Walters is sending us home."

"I'm sorry about Moose. I know he's your friend, and you're trying to help him. But that doesn't mean you have to leave with him. You and I have been the best of enemies for eight years. You can't just quit before we finish the contest."

"Sorry."

"But camp's over tomorrow. You can see Moose then and talk to him all you want."

"It's complicated."

"So you're just going to quit?"

"Yep."

Meadow eased into our conversation. I asked her if she had seen Pastor Mac.

"I think he's back by the dorms where his truck is parked. I hear you're leaving."

"I guess so. The skunk hair was just too much for Dr. Walters. He said we have to leave."

"You too?"

"Well, no, but Moose has to go. I'm leaving with him."

"But what about the rest of your team? We need you too."

I checked my watch. Time was running out. "I've been here all week and right now we're at rock bottom. I think you can lose just fine without me. I'm sorry to leave you with the toilets, but if it will help I'll eat a peanut butter sandwich for supper."

Meadow folded her arms. "Eureka's not over yet. We haven't gotten some of our points. Then there's this afternoon's activity. We still have a chance. We might not win, but we won't necessarily get last place either."

I started walking toward the dorms. "So I'm supposed to blow Moose off so our team can eat beanie-wienies instead of peanut butter sandwiches?"

"OK. We probably won't win or come close to it. But we can finish well, with our heads held high. Isn't that what you've been telling us all week? You're our captain. We need you."

99

"You take my place. You always seem to know what to say. Not me. I never have the answers when I need them."

"No one has all the answers, Cody. But you keep everyone working when things look hopeless. You don't quit—until now."

"Look, Meadow, I don't expect you to understand. But is there one Christian friend who always stood by you when you first became a Christian? One person who helped you through the tough times?"

"Well, my pastor's wife led me to the Lord. I had a hard time leaving behind our traditional religion to do things the Christian way. Sometimes I threw some pretty weird questions and arguments at her. She couldn't always explain things in a way I could understand, but she didn't give up on me either. She allowed me time to grow."

"Well, this is a critical time for Moose, and I'm trying to be the friend who makes a difference. I'm sorry if it looks like I'm quitting on you guys, but I have to choose between quitting on you or quitting on Moose. He needs me more." I could see Pastor Mac by his truck. I stopped so Meadow wouldn't follow me. "Tell everyone I'm sorry, OK?"

"No, I won't do that. I guess you have your reasons for leaving, but if you want our team to understand, you'll have to tell them yourself. I won't make excuses for you."

I left her standing by the dorm and headed towards Pastor Mac. He tossed some muddy boots into the back of his truck as I walked up.

"I guess you heard about the skunk hair incident," I said.

"Yep."

"Dr. Walters is sending Moose home."

"I'm sorry about that."

"It's not fair! OK, Moose has done some things he shouldn't have. But Wesley's no saint either. He's constantly challenging everything Moose says. When he told the entire camp what Moose's name is, he really hurt Moose. I didn't even know Moose's real name was Malcolm. Wesley never gets told off because he knows which no-noes are socially acceptable and which will get him

in trouble. But Dr. Walters isn't about to forgive Moose for anything."

"Actually Dr. Walters has warned Moose several times."

"He doesn't understand people like Moose, does he? He doesn't
know what it's like to be saved out of a rough family with friends
who are always in trouble."

Pastor Mac handed me a cinnamon roll from the front seat.
He must have begged them off the cooks when he realized Moose
and I didn't get breakfast. "His dad was a pastor. He hasn't expe-
rienced what it's like to live a sinful lifestyle far from God. That's
good, you know."

"I know," I muttered. "But it doesn't help him understand
Moose."

He leaned against the dirty truck. "I guess it's a little easier
for me to understand Moose. I got into smoking and drinking
like Moose. I did some things I regret now. Sin is never worth it,
Cody.

"Even though I'm a pastor, I face the natural consequences
for the drinking and smoking I did as a teen. I thank the Lord,
however, that God kept me away from some sins that could have
kept me from the ministry. You should thank the Lord every day
that he has protected you from the life of sin that Moose has had
to endure. You can see in Moose how that past sin hinders his
spiritual growth now."

"I know that. I just wish Dr. Walters would be more sympa-
thetic. He thinks Moose is being so bad. He should have seen
Moose before he was saved. He was the most obnoxious, foulmouthed guy at our school. Moose has really come a long way. It
wasn't easy for him to come to camp. He's even getting discouraged about going to church because people get impatient with all
the stuff he has to learn."

I told Pastor Mac about our deal. "Moose has really tried this
week, Pastor Mac, and it kills me to think what it's going to do to
him to have him kicked out of camp."

"I understand that. You're a good friend, Cody."

I took a bite of the roll and licked the frosting off my hands.
"Dr. Walters is always talking about rules and the consequences

of breaking them. It didn't used to be like that. When you were camp dean, you didn't talk about rules all the time."

"I suppose Dr. Walters and I have different styles of running things."

"Right. I like your way better. You care about people more than rules."

"Back your truck up, Cody, and step on the brakes. We've had some good years at camp. We've had easy years when most of the kids were Christians who got along well together. You and Luke were always squabbling about who would win, but it was just friendly competition. No one got hurt. When you've got fairly mature Christians who are nice to each other, you don't need many rules. This has not been one of those easy years. Don't assume Dr. Walters doesn't care about people just because he enforces the rules."

"But if Moose gets sent home early, he might never go to church again! Can't you talk to Dr. Walters and get him to change his mind?"

"Nope. He's the camp dean. I'm not going to challenge his authority."

"But what he's doing to Moose is not right!"

"He has every right to send Moose home. Moose has done some serious things. Dr. Walters warned him, but Moose kept pushing it."

"If you were camp dean, would you send Moose home?"

"I'm not camp dean. I don't think you need to know that."

"So there's nothing I can do about it?"

"I didn't say that. You could go and talk to Dr. Walters."

He had to be joking. "Me? He would never listen to me."

"In your present mood, no. But remember Daniel?"

"Yep. The king made a bad law. Daniel refused to obey it. And now it's like Moose is being thrown to the lions because Wesley and Dr. Walters show no mercy. All this stuff is going to destroy Moose!"

"Actually I was thinking about an incident earlier in Daniel's life. He was commanded to eat the king's food which had been offered to idols and probably included food the Jews weren't allowed to eat. What did he do?"

"He refused to eat it."

"Yep. But look at the way he refused."

I frowned. I had read Daniel before. Daniel refused to do wrong even though it was hard. We needed to determine to obey God no matter what. That was the whole point, wasn't it? Was there more? Pastor Mac waited while I ate half my cinnamon roll.

"Remember my sermon last night?"

"Yep. You talked about targets. I feel like a target this week. Moose too. Everyone is aiming at us."

"I also talked about aiming to do God's will and not letting anything keep us from hitting the target. I've watched you grow in Christ from one year at camp to the next. But Cody, this is a dangerous time for you. Or it could be a step of growth. Read Daniel one again. Look at the respectful way Daniel approached authority and asked for a change in diet. If you go to Dr. Walters with an attitude like that, who knows what will happen?"

"But I already talked to him. He wouldn't listen."

Pastor Mac shrugged. "Maybe not. But I volunteered to take Moose home. I can't leave until after chapel this morning. That gives you a couple of hours."

"I'm going with him. I don't know if it'll help or not, but I can't bear to see him leave alone without anyone to help him think things through."

"I understand. I don't know if you would change Pastor Walter's mind by talking to him, but as far as I can see, it's your only chance."

I didn't understand everything Pastor Mac was trying to say. But if there was a chance to turn this thing around, I had to try. I took my Bible to the far side of camp and found a tree trunk to sit on. I read Daniel one. Pastor Mac seemed to think the answer was in this chapter. What was it?

Daniel refused to eat the food.

"Dr. Walters," I could say. "Your decision to make Moose leave camp is bad, wrong, destructive. I refuse to accept it. You've got to let Moose stay!"

Nope. That would never work. Daniel was polite, respectful. I skimmed the chapter again.

"Please, Dr. Walters! Give Moose one more chance! I beg you! I plead with you! I'll do anything, just don't send him home!"

Nope. Daniel didn't beg. He asked permission. When that didn't work he suggested a creative alternative to the orders and asked to have a chance to prove himself.

What kind of creative alternative could there be to sending Moose home? I pulled the multi-tool out of my pocket and stared at it, as if the answer were written there. Pliers, screwdriver, knife, bottle opener, ruler, wire stripper. How could I fix this?

Bottle opener. I could open up to Dr. Walters and share my heart. Ruler. I could measure his reaction. Wire stripper. I could strip away all his objections. Screwdriver. Maybe I should really put the screws on him. Knife. This was ridiculous.

I shoved the multi-tool back in my pocket.

Moose didn't care if he got sent home. I was the one who cared. If only I could think of something I could do to spare Moose. Jesus died in our place. Could I be a substitute for Moose? Substitute punishment was a biblical concept. It might work!

I prayed a little and thought some more. Then I checked my watch. Time for chapel.

Moose met me at the door. "Where have you been? I went to the dorm to hunt for something to eat and never saw you again. Have you been hiding?"

"Nope. Just had something I had to work on before we leave."

I mumbled the songs and didn't get anything out of Pastor Mac's sermon. I figured my personal sermon from him was more important.

After chapel I cornered Dr. Walters and asked to talk to him. I waited until the chapel was empty to begin.

"Dr. Walters, I know what Moose did really upset Wesley. You're the camp dean, and you have a right to send him home."

Dr. Walters just waited.

"I know Moose rubs people the wrong way, but he isn't trying to make people mad. Moose's family is really a mess. He's a new Christian, and he's come a long way since he was saved four months ago. He still has a long way to go, but he is trying. I honestly believe he thought bleaching Wesley's hair was an innocent joke. He meant to tease Wesley, not hurt him."

"Well, whether or not he meant to, his actions had that result."

"I know that. To Wesley, having bleached hair makes him feel worldly, like an unbeliever. It makes him feel not only stupid, but wrong. But honestly, I think if you did something to Moose's hair, he'd just shrug it off. Moose has a hard time keeping rules. Wesley, on the other hand, is an absolute expert at keeping rules, so everyone thinks he's this great Christian. But Wesley hasn't exactly been Mr. Nice Guy this week. He just doesn't get into trouble because he knows which sins are socially acceptable at Bible camp. I guess it doesn't hurt to be the dean's son either."

Dr. Walters sighed. "Cody, don't be too quick to think you know the inside of a person when you can only see the outside. There was a man back in Tennessee who was a model citizen. He obeyed all the laws and never got into trouble. But the promotion he thought he deserved was given to a woman. He fed his jealousy and hatred until it was boiling, but he never broke a law. Then one day he took a gun, drove to her house and shot her dead. Before he killed the woman, his heart was chock full of hatred and meanness, but you can't arrest a man for thinking mean thoughts."

"So what you're trying to say is: We don't know what Moose and Wesley are really thinking so we shouldn't judge them?"

"What I'm trying to say is: You think I'm showing Wesley preferential treatment because I'm punishing Moose and not Wesley. Moose has spent the week pushing the boundaries. He committed several serious offenses. After all of that, we warned him, gave him one last chance. He still bleached Wesley's hair. Wesley is not just my son. He is a camper. Moose went way too far with his hair and really hurt him. Meanwhile, I don't know of one rule that Wesley has broken. We don't send campers home for what we think might be in their hearts. We send them home when they keep breaking the rules and challenge authority. It doesn't have anything to do with the fact that Wesley is my son."

"Sorry. I shouldn't have said that about Wesley being your son. I'm just really worried about Moose. He looks tough, but he's like a crystal goblet spiritually. If you send him home now, this way, I think it will make him turn away from the church and God."

"We can't see Moose's heart and tell what he needs. Maybe he needs to know that wrong actions bring bad consequences."

"OK. He deserves to be sent home. You want to do this so others will understand this kind of behavior will not be tolerated. I, myself, deserve hell. God demands punishment for sin. But God also loves to show mercy. So Jesus took my punishment, and God said that was good enough. I want to bear Moose's punishment. Send me home instead."

Dr. Walters studied my face. "Cody, I know you want to help your friend, but if I send you home that still leaves us with Moose. I don't think I can trust him to show appropriate behavior when he doesn't even know what that is."

"Then give me another punishment. I'll stay after camp and clean out the rain gutters. I can scrub out the dumpster and fix the broken board on the fence. If there's a way to clean up the soccer field after that flour and water game, I'll do it. Punish me, but let Moose finish camp. We only have one day of camp left."

"Listen. You may be trying to do the right thing here, but you care so much about Moose you are not thinking clearly. I have been more lenient than usual with Moose. After repeated warnings and offenses he humiliated a camper who just happens to be my son. Can you give me one good reason why I should not follow through with the consequences?"

The only reason I could think of was that I didn't want him to. I didn't think that counted. I shook my head. "Guess he'll have to leave. Think I'll go with him."

"Don't let this pull you down, Cody. Rebellion can be contagious."

"I'm not trying to be rebellious. I just think Moose needs a friend to go with him and work things out."

I turned to walk away, but Dr. Walters stopped me. "For the record," he said, "you can obey all the rules and still have a heart which is far from God. But I have never met anyone who had a very close walk with the Lord who continually struggled with authority issues."

I shuffled to the door. Wesley was hovering around it, like a junior camp dean checking up on his dad. He had found a green cap somewhere that read "Sure Value Hardware" and used it to cover the damage. I looked him straight in the eye. "Well, Wesley, you win. Moose and I are leaving."

Worry covered Wesley's face. "Dad's not making *you* leave, is he? It's not your fault Moose stirs up trouble and ruins everything our team tries to do."

I shook my head. "You still don't get it, do you? You don't know what it means to care so much about a friend that you would do almost anything to keep him from getting hurt."

I found Moose in the dorm stuffing things into his giant bag. "Took you long enough," he said.

"Yep. Just getting ready to go." I held up a dirty sock. "This yours?"

Moose smelled it. "Nah. Must belong to someone else. Look, Cody, you don't have to go home just because I messed up. I don't fit in at this stupid Bible camp, but you do. Why should you leave?"

I grabbed my sports bag and started stuffing things inside. "Don't worry about it. I wouldn't be much good at camp without you anyway."

"So what are you going to do? Baby-sit me? Try to get me to go back on our deal?"

"Hey, a deal's a deal. If you don't want to go to church, I'm not going to make you. I wanted camp to be good for you. I wish I could go ahead of you and make life fair and right and good. But sometimes life just isn't what you want it to be. You've got to decide if you're going to let the bad stuff keep you from serving the Lord or not. I can't do it for you."

"So how come you're leaving with me?"

I turned away from him and wiped my eyes. "It's just something I've got to do."

"You've had eight years of camp here. If there was an award for best all-around camper, you'd get it. You've got four other team members counting on you, and this is your last chance to show Luke up. Why would you leave all that behind?"

107

"Doesn't matter. You're not going to talk me out of leaving, so you might as well save your breath."

"It's like Mrs. Grumball, isn't it? We washed her car because we wanted her rose. You think if you leave camp early with me, maybe I'll listen to you. Maybe I'll go back to church and become a decent Christian some day."

"Don't psychoanalyze me. I'm leaving because I want to leave. Check under the bunks and make sure we got everything."

"You would leave all this behind in the off chance that it might make a difference in my Christian life?"

I glared at him. "Yes," I shouted. "What do you think I've been doing for the last four months?"

I snatched a couple of shirts off of their clothes hooks and shoved them into my bag. I had to keep myself angry, or I would cry.

Moose's eyes followed my every move. "No one ever did anything like that for me before."

I zipped up my sleeping bag, rolled it, and pulled the tie around the middle.

"Y'all can quit packing." It was Wesley in his green cap. When did he come in? He must have tiptoed. "We've got one last chance to win, and we're way behind now. You better run down to the climbing wall and take your turn. Then don't you think we ought to use the half hour before lunch to work out some kind of strategy?"

I stared at Wesley. My mouth was probably hanging open too. "What do you mean? Your dad said we had to go. Well, he said Moose had to go, and if Moose goes, I go."

"I know. But if you leave, we lose our captain. We don't need Moose, but we need you. Since Eureka is all about teamwork, Pastor Steve would probably deduct a lot of points for breaking up the team too. You leave, we lose. I don't want to lose."

"But your dad said—"

"I talked to my dad. What Moose did hurt me, no one else. If I say he stays, what's the point of sending him home?"

Moose grinned. "Hey, Wesley. You're not as bad as I thought you were."

Wesley glared at Moose. "Don't push it," he muttered. "I'll go tell the team to meet at the candy shack in fifteen minutes."

Wesley walked out. I stared at the empty doorframe. Maybe Dr. Walters really was looking for one good reason not to send Moose home. I didn't understand how or when or why. But somehow Wesley had handed us something no one else could give—a second chance.

13

I couldn't believe it. Just hours ago an irate Wesley had ratted on Moose. By the time he was done his dad had decided Moose didn't belong at camp and demanded he be sent home. Now Wesley had asked his dad to reverse his decision so Moose and I could stay. Why? I couldn't believe Wesley actually cared that much about winning. Maybe God was working in his heart too.

Of course, I could have hoped for more. I could have hoped for an apology like: "I'm sorry. I was wrong. Moose was wrong too, but I overreacted." Something like that. But sometimes older Christians had a harder time admitting they were wrong than new Christians. Why was that?

Now we had a second chance—if not to win, at least to finish with dignity. God was giving me a second chance too, to be a real captain. I had stumbled through the week not knowing what to do or say half of the time. Now our team needed leadership more than ever. In all of our defeat there had to be some sort of way to lead them to victory.

Moose unrolled his sleeping bag and threw his sports bag in the corner. "So, Captain Cody, are you going to stand there or are we going to figure out how to get something better than PBJ sandwiches out of this deal?"

Moose and I ran to the climbing wall just as the others were finishing up. Pastor Steve called this activity Joshua's Spies. Teams didn't compete in wall-climbing, but everyone was supposed to try, so we had to do our bit. Then we raced to the candy shack where we found a dejected group of Grizzlies. Some were leaning on the shack. Some were sitting on a bench beside it.

I found a spot somewhat front and center to the group and pulled myself to the full amount of what little height I had. "OK, team, I am your captain, and I've got something to say."

Meadow said, "I thought you were leaving."

"Well, we're not. So as I was saying, we are the Grizzlies. Some may say we're a miserable bunch of misfits who can't work together. They are glad to let us eat their peanut butter sandwiches and clean their toilets. But I say they're wrong.

"Sure we have our differences, but if we work together, who knows what we can do? We've got one more afternoon. I don't think we have a smell of a chance to win first place. We'd have to get some mega bonus points to do that. But if we work hard, we won't be eating PBJ sandwiches either."

Tana twirled a red curl around her finger. "I hate to boo the cheerleaders, Cody, but would it be so terrible if we lost? I mean, someone's got to lose and PBJs aren't that bad."

I thought about that one. A good coach would inspire them to win, but maybe I should just share my heart. "Losing is not the end of the world. I've lost my share of ballgames and then some. But whatever we do, I want to finish well. So far this week we've been losers all apart from how the other teams are doing. Instead of competing with other teams, we've turned on each other. We haven't tried our hardest. We've lost the respect of other teams. And we've lost the smile of God. That's just not good enough.

"I say for one last afternoon let's work together as a team and give it our absolute best. Surely we can do better than last place. But whatever happens, when we cross the finish line . . ." I drew a line in the dirt with my toe. "I want us to feel like winners, no matter what place we get in the contest."

Bench sitters sat up. Wall leaners forgot to slouch. Newfound hope shone from their eyes.

Titus stepped forward. He was holding a list of our points so far. "We've got to win this afternoon's event. We've still got the Montana Map and the Montana Treasures. Today we get the points for them. Looks like we'll have over three hundred points for the map, but most of the other teams will do well on that too."

He added the three hundred to his list. "We've got to really work on the treasures. At fifty points apiece they could make the difference."

"Titus is right," I said. "If we get some bonus points and extra points for teamwork, we might still have a chance to finish in some respectable position."

Moose pushed the cowboy hat back on his head. "Gourmet pizza and huckleberry pie would suit me fine."

I wasn't going to hold out for winning first place. That would take a minor miracle. But if Moose wanted to push for that, I wouldn't stop him.

"OK, Tana and Meadow. What's that cheer you made up? We're going to need it."

The girls led the cheer. "Owls hoot, Coyotes howl. Elk bugle, Grizzlies growl. Bobcats purr and Cougars scream. We're the best, the Grizzly team!"

"Do cougars really scream?" I asked.

"The females do," Meadow said. "My uncle heard one once. He said his heart pounded for two weeks after that."

"Well, we're Grizzlies, and we'd better start growling."

The lunch bell rang. The others headed toward the dining hall. Meadow caught my eye. She smiled. "Welcome back, Captain."

The Grizzlies sat together for lunch. We wolfed down some hamburgers. While other tables joked and laughed, we talked about the afternoon activity and where Pastor Steve would take us. Would it be a good place to find treasures for the contest? I had never felt so competitive in my life.

Finally Pastor Steve stood up. "This afternoon we have one final event. We call it Moses's Famous Walk. About a half mile from here is the beginning of a nice hiking trail that takes you to the top of a mountain we're going to call Mount Sinai. Pastor Mac has already climbed to the top and left a stone shaped like the ten commandments. All of you are going to be Moses and climb to the top of Mt. Sinai to reach it. The first person from each team to reach the top will sign the ten commandments rock for his team and take a picture of the whole rock. The first team to sign the rock will get one thousand two hundred points, second team one thousand, and so on down to two hundred points. Now eventually every team member must climb to the top and sign the rock, but points will be given according to the first one on your team to reach the ten commandments. When all of your team has reached the top, take a picture by the rock to show that you were all there."

Perfect. We'd give Meadow the camera, and we'd be sure to get first place.

"On the way down the mountain take your time. You have plenty of time to make it, so this would be a good time to find any items you still lack on your Montana Treasures list. Be sure not to get so far from the trail that you get lost, however. We'll have counselors hiking with us, but some of you know Montana better than they do. You shouldn't have any problems, but if you should happen to lose the trail, follow the river. The trail and river both lead you back to the trail head where the vehicles park. From the trail head you need to walk back to camp. The camp gate is your finish line."

Luke raised his hand. "Do we get more points for getting back to camp early?"

"No. Arriving at the top of the mountain is what gives you points. You can come back to camp any time you want. But every team member must be back at camp by six o'clock. If you are late your team loses one thousand points."

Tana raised her hand. "What if we're really late?"

"We'll just say that for every hour you are late, you will lose another one thousand points. We don't want to mess up dinner time for the cooks. So take your time coming down, find the treasures on your list, have fun. But make sure every team member is back at camp by six o'clock. Every team member must reach the top of Mt. Sinai and cross the finish line at camp or your team loses Eureka."

Our team was first into the vehicles, ready to go. Luke climbed in behind us. He grinned. "What's with you guys? You act like you're gonna win or something. Have you forgotten that you were in last place just last night?"

"That was yesterday," I said. "Today we get all the points from the Treasures and Bible Map. Today we are motivated. Today you

Coyotes better watch out because, who knows? We just might beat you."

Luke laughed. "You're kidding! You think you have a chance of beating us? You think you might actually win?"

Actually I didn't, but I was captain and my teammates were listening. "You never know what might happen. If I were you, I'd be worried. You just might lose your huckleberry pie."

"You don't have a chance. You have been trying to beat me for eight years, Cody Boedecker. But this year the winner takes all. This year we find out who the real champion is."

"I can see why you'd be worried."

"I think you forget who's ahead so far and who's in last place."

"I think you underestimate us."

Luke thought for a minute. "Tell you what. If you win, if the Grizzlies actually make up all those points and beat the Coyotes and come in first, I will personally write 'Cody is champ' on my pillow case and run it up the flagpole."

"Hope your mom doesn't get mad."

I was glad when we got to the trail head. Who knows what I would be promising if Luke kept on taunting me?

We jumped out of the vehicles, and Meadow took off like the wind. Luke wasn't far behind her. The rest of the campers started up the trail. Soon speed and stamina, or lack thereof, sorted everyone into hiking groups. Moose, Wesley, Titus, and I walked near the front. Tana hung back with some girls from other teams.

"I wish Tana would hurry up," Titus complained.

"Never mind," I said. "Meadow is sure to grab first place for us. We'll have plenty of time coming down to search for Montana treasures."

We kept a steady pace for about an hour and a half. When we reached the top, Luke stood by the ten commandments grinning.

I glanced around. "Where's Meadow?"

"What's the problem?" Luke teased. "You Grizzlies don't have any chance of winning anyway—unless you call sixth place winning."

"But she was ahead of us at the trail head."

Meadow's voice startled me from behind. "Don't listen to Luke. We got first place. I've just been hunting for some of the stuff on the list. Here's the marker. Don't forget to sign the rock."

We took the marker from Meadow and signed our names. Other groups started to appear. People snapped pictures of the rock and admired the view.

Titus checked his watch. "It's three o'clock. Where's Tana?"

"Relax," Meadow whispered. "No one else has started down yet, and I think we should be last to leave. I have a plan."

That sounded promising.

Finally Tana turned up with a couple of girls and Mrs. Burkhart, the pastor's wife from Polson. "Sorry it took me so long," Tana said. "These hiking boots are new. They were wearing a sore on my little toes, and I had to stop and put Band-Aids on them."

Meadow encouraged Tana to take off her boots and air out her feet. The various groups started down the trail. When the last group but us got ready to go, Mrs. Burkhart turned to us. "Are you ready to go?" she said. "I'm bringing up the rear."

"We're walking off the trail for a little ways to find Montana treasures," Meadow said. "Don't tell anyone. We'll join the trail before long."

"Well, OK. Just don't get lost."

"Don't worry. My dad takes me hunting all the time, and I never get lost. I think I saw a shortcut on the way up. We'll probably beat you back to camp."

Mrs. Burkhart waved goodbye and sped down the trail to catch up to the others.

Tana handed out granola bars.

Meadow said, "We need animals, right?" She checked the Montana Bible Treasures list. "A bat, a bear or fox, a goat or sheep, which could be a mountain goat or sheep, our cougar, a mouse, snake, wolf, or weasel. Then there are the birds. Crow, eagle, owl, pigeon, quail. Even a bee would help."

Moose shook his head. "Fat chance of us finding many of those."

"We won't find many of them," Meadow agreed. "But we could possibly find any one of them. And if we brought back a picture of

115

a mountain goat or bear, I'm sure Pastor Steve would find a way to give bonus points for that."

Moose leaned back on a rock and pulled his cowboy hat down low over his eyes. "So how are we going to get these great pictures?"

"Well, Moose, you're a hunter. Right now about thirty campers and a few adults are stomping down the trail, chasing all the animals away. Where do we need to be?"

Moose pointed down the mountain. "If I was hunting, I'd sneak down that draw over there and wait for the animals to come to me."

"Exactly. We haven't got all day, but how about if we head down that draw, quietly, looking for animals? We can find a comfy spot and sit for about twenty minutes and see what we find."

I shrugged. "Why not? It's the best chance we've got. If it doesn't work, we'll just hike back to the trail."

This time we made our own trail. At first we dodged tree branches. Pine and fir needles carpeted the path. Soon, however, we were forced to climb around rocks and work our way through dense undergrowth.

Before long we found rock seats in a thick group of pine trees. Titus held the camera ready to snap. We listened to bird calls and branches shaking in the breeze. I breathed in the scent of pine trees. Wesley coughed. Moose shushed him.

"What if a cougar sneaks up on us?" Wesley asked.

"Would you stop with the cougars for once?" Moose snapped. "Cougars don't sneak up on people. They avoid people altogether. You're lucky if you see one."

"But Pastor Mac said cougars stalk people and pounce on them."

"Only if they're hungry or you come between them and their young. No cougar is going to attack six full-grown teenagers."

"What about bears?"

"Same thing. Now shush!"

Suddenly leaves rustled. We all jumped in our seats. I almost fell off my rock. A chipmunk scurried out to us, then made a quick retreat.

Moose shook his head. "You and your cougar!"

A magpie swooped by. Something buzzed. A bee landed on an Indian paintbrush wildflower. Five of us pointed frantically while Titus snapped the picture.

"Missed it." Titus jumped up.

The bee buzzed off, spiraling and zigzagging its way. Titus spiraled and zigzagged with it, snapping all the way.

"Got it!" he announced as he took his seat again. "Hey, it's not a bear, but it's fifty points."

Silently we listened to nature, searching the landscape for the slightest movement. Again leaves rustled. This time a field mouse stuck his nose out of a hole near Moose. Titus immediately snapped the picture. The field mouse sped off.

Moose picked up a big rock. "The samples don't have to be alive. I could get an extra fifty points."

"Forget it," Meadow shouted, scaring the mouse back into his hole. "His life is worth more than fifty points."

We had gained one hundred points and decided it was time to go.

"We still need the bitterroot flower," Tana reminded us. "And a thistle. Maybe we can find one of them."

The ground was rocky now, and we were picking our way slowly, but we would make up time on the trail. After about fifteen minutes Tana announced, "I see pink!"

Our eyes scanned the area searching for color. "Where?"

She pointed just over a rise. "You have to stand on this rock. Then you can see it."

We scurried to the pink patch. Lewis monkey flowers. Nice, but not Bible flowers.

Then Wesley spotted a patch. "Are these bitterroot flowers?" he asked. But when we drew closer, we could see that they were just those pinky daisies you see in the mountains.

Once we began looking for them, we kept seeing pink everywhere. We even found some tiny Calypso orchids, but no bitterroot. I realized then that it was four o'clock. We'd better find the trail and get moving.

Titus found a trail that would likely join the main trail. Meadow led the way for about half an hour. Then she stopped so quickly that Titus ran into her.

She ran her fingers through her hair. "Whew! Uh, team, I don't think this is the right trail."

We slipped up beside her. She was standing at the edge of a four foot drop-off, hidden by dense undergrowth. Whatever animal made this trail must have had a good set of brakes. We turned in every direction, hoping to spot a trail, any trail that led somewhere this trail didn't.

"Look!" Tana exclaimed.

"What?" I asked.

"A thistle. We still need a thistle for our list."

Thistles were the farthest thing from my mind right then, but I pulled out my multi-tool and handed it to Tana. Titus snapped the picture, and Tana worked the prickly thing out with the screwdriver. She fished a plastic bag out of her backpack and put the thistle inside. No one even remarked about the extra hundred points we'd get. Everyone but Tana was too busy looking for trails.

Moose pointed off to one side. "See that little deer trail? I bet it's a shortcut to the main trail."

Since no one had a better suggestion, we followed Moose's trail. After about fifteen minutes, however, the trail dwindled to nothing. We climbed to the top of a huge rock to get our bearings, but the camp and the lake hid behind a rise in the distance.

"Something's wrong," Meadow warned. "I can feel it."

"You're right about that." I said. "We're lost."

Meadow shook her head. "But we shouldn't be lost. The main trail and the creek both run down the mountain. The river runs east of the trail. At the top of the mountain we headed downhill and east. With all our walking, how come we never hit the river?"

"Maybe we didn't go far enough," Moose suggested.

"Then how come we never hit the main trail? We've been walking this way a long time."

"Maybe we've been going in circles between the two," Titus suggested.

"Could we have crossed the creek without knowing it?" I asked.

"I think we'd know it if we crossed a creek. Maybe we crossed the main trail and didn't know it."

"The main trail is pretty obvious," Moose pointed out.

Tana sat on a log. "Not everywhere. On the way up I sat on some big rocks to put Band-Aids on my toes. It was on this wide, flat area that was so flat that any of it could be part of a trail or just an open area. We could have passed the trail at a place like that and never noticed."

Meadow searched the sky. "It's too bad you can't see the sun. When does Montana ever have thick cloud cover like this in August?"

"It doesn't matter where the sun is. Camp is that way." Moose pointed to a spot over the horizon.

"It can't be that direction," Meadow told him. "That's too far west."

Titus pointed off a different direction. "I'd say camp is right over there."

"You're all wrong. Camp is that way." Tana pointed in yet another direction.

Everyone stared at Tana. Like we would take her word for it.

"It is. See that little pink patch?" Tana pointed to a tiny splotch in the direction she thought camp should be. "That's the roof of a little girl's tree house just down the road from camp."

"You have a thing for pink, don't you?" Moose asked. "That pink spot could be anything."

"But it's not anything. It's the tree house. And it's the right direction." She glanced from person to person, meeting nothing but skepticism. "I've got a great sense of direction. I can shop for hours in a mall and never get lost. Even an out-of-state mall."

"You may be a great shopper, but camp is that way." Moose pointed his direction.

"No, it's not. It's that way." Titus pointed his direction.

"I really think it's somewhere in between," Meadow added.

I couldn't believe it. Four of us grew up in Montana. Three of us were hunters. We hiked two hours up a mountain with an obvious main trail and came down between the trail and a creek. It made no sense at all. But one thing was sure—we were lost.

If we all had different ideas about what direction camp was, we would also have different ideas about what to do next. We didn't need more ideas, we needed decisive leadership. I was captain, so I was it.

"Look. We've got to think this through," I said. "We can't all be right. Actually we can't all be wrong either for all the different directions we're pointing in. We've got to find a trail. Any trail will lead us back to civilization. Well, OK, maybe a deer trail won't, but any people trail will. If the trail doesn't lead us near camp, we'll call camp from wherever we end up. Tana, hand me that purple hair thing you've been readjusting all day."

Tana pulled the tie from her hair and handed it to me.

"I'm going to tie this to this pine tree by this big rock so we can all find our way back. Let's all go in different directions and look for a trail or the creek. Meet back here in five minutes, no more. If you find a trail, yell eureka!"

Three minutes later I heard an "ow" from Wesley's direction. I headed that way.

"Wesley, is that you? Did you find something? You're supposed to yell eureka, not ow."

A voice came from nowhere. "Help! I'm over here."

Soon the other five had gathered and were searching for Wesley. We could see trees and rocks everywhere, but no Wesley.

I yelled again. "Over where? Wesley, where are you?"

The voice drifted up to us from a ring of trees and bushes. "I'm down here. Watch your step. It drops off suddenly, and the side is crumbling."

We crept over to the trees. They bordered a horseshoe-shaped drop-off which formed one end of a deep ravine hidden in the thick forest. We inched up to the edge. Wesley was right. The edge was crumbling.

I grabbed a tree which grew out over the edge and swung around until I could see our lost team member. Wesley was hanging onto a little sapling that grew out of the sides of the drop-off about fifteen feet down. His cap had fallen down the ravine onto the rocks below.

Moose found a tree and hung over the scene too. "Wesley, what are you doing? There are no trails down there."

"I kind of figured that out, Moose. I didn't really come down here on purpose. You want to help me out?"

"Well, I don't know, Wesley. Since God controls everything, I think I'll let Him help you out."

"Moose! My arms are giving out!"

"Guess you better pray and ask God to rescue you."

"Well, I'm sure He could send an angel from heaven, but why would He do that when you're standing there doing nothing?"

"Why Wesley, do you need my help? I thought you didn't want my help."

"Just pull me out of here, would you?"

After a whole week of camp, these two were still bickering. I had hoped that, as Christians, they would call a truce and work together. After Wesley had asked his dad to let Moose stay, I had hoped Moose and Wesley would patch things up and do more than tolerate each other. Actually I had had lots of hopes, and they had all come down to this. Wesley had to talk Moose into saving his life. What a disaster!

Or was it? Maybe this disaster offered opportunity as well.

"Wesley," I said. "Find yourself a solid foothold."

"Where?"

"Anywhere. Kick a hole in the dirt if you have to. You're going to need a foothold. You might as well get comfortable, because it's going to take us a while to figure out how to get you out of there."

Wesley kicked dirt from around the rocky protrusion he was perched on until he could take most of the weight off his arms. "Well, I'm glad someone cares enough to help me out of here."

"You're right, Wesley. We all care," I called down to him. "But only Moose is strong enough to pull you up. So the first thing you guys are gonna do is settle your differences."

"Could you pull me up first?

"Nope. Don't think that'll work. See, Moose is pretty stubborn, and I've never been able to get him to do anything he didn't want to do. And if there's anyone more stubborn than Moose, it's you. I figure you guys deserve each other. You don't like teaming up with Moose because he's obnoxious and doesn't fit into Christian stuff. He doesn't like you because you're a spiritual snob and don't fit into Montana.

"But like it or not you're on the same team. More than that you're both Christians. So why don't you guys apologize to each other so we can figure out how to get you out of there?"

"But I'm no good at apologies!" Wesley whined.

"Then this is a good time to practice."

Wesley rested one arm while he held on to the sapling with the other. "OK, OK. Moose, I know I've messed up this week, and I'm sorry. You want to pull me up?"

"Do you really mean that, Wesley?" Moose taunted. "Or are you just saying that to save your skin?"

"Yes, I mean it! I've been wanting to say something anyway. Really! But I was looking for a better time—like sometime when our whole team isn't listening, and I'm not about to drop into an abyss. All right. Sometimes I act like I a total jerk, but really I am totally lost in Montana. Nothing I know how to do seems to matter here."

"Then you know how I feel when I can't make any sense of Bible stuff and what people expect Christians to do," Moose told him.

Wesley shifted his weight to his other arm. "Yes, sir. I do. So I should have been the first one to be a true friend. I blew it. I actually think we could help each other a lot if we would, and this would be a stupendous time to start. I really need your help to get out of here."

"Pardon me?" Moose called. "I don't think I heard you Wesley."

"I need your help."

"What was that?"

"Come on, Malcolm, help me out here."

122

Moose laughed. "All right, Skunky, I'll try. I guess I've been a little hard on you too. But you're an awful long ways down there. How do you suggest I get you out of there?"

"You want to throw me a rope or something?"

"Great idea, Wes. Stupendous idea. Now where am I supposed to get rope?"

Tana suddenly spoke up. "You need rope? I can help with that one."

I swung my weight back to solid ground. "Don't tell me you've got a rope in your backpack!"

"Well, not a rope really, but I've got the cord on my backpack. And I've got a jacket with a hood on it. The hood has a cord, and the bottom does too. If we tied them together . . ."

"I'll tie the knots," Titus said.

"Dump that backpack, girl!" Meadow shouted.

Tana dumped.

Wesley's voice drifted up to us. "Hey guys, I think I see eyes down here. There's something hiding in the brush."

"Come on, Wes," Moose growled. "You've been seeing cougars all week. It's probably just another chipmunk."

"I don't know. Those eyes look pretty big. And look. There are some kittens with little spots. It's weird. They sound like they're whistling."

Meadow darted to the edge of the drop-off. "It's a cougar! Really, look!" She pointed down the ravine. "Below Wesley in those bushes. There's Mama Cougar!"

14

"Smile, Wesley!" Meadow yelled. "Look at the cougar and smile."

"You've got to be joking!"

"No. Smile. Show your teeth. Keep looking at her. Don't turn your back."

Moose, Titus, and I each grabbed a cord from Tana's stuff and yanked it out of the item it belonged to. Titus knotted the cords into one long one, testing the strength of each connection.

"Tie the cord to my ankle," Moose demanded.

Titus looked confused, but obeyed.

Moose circled the tree trunk with his arms and locked his arms. He swung his body over the edge.

"Grab the rope," he yelled to Wesley.

Meanwhile Meadow had picked up a large tree branch and was waving it frantically over the side of the drop-off. She yelled to Tana to do the same.

"Grab my arms," Moose ordered Titus and me.

I grabbed hold of Moose's arm and laid flat on my belly for the best weight distribution.

"Titus, where are you?" I called.

A camera clicked. Then Titus latched onto Moose's other arm. "I couldn't miss a shot like that," he explained. "We'll win the teamwork prize for sure!"

"Keep looking at her, Wesley!" Meadow shouted. "Growl at her, yell, make some kind of noise."

"Hey, cat! Scram!" Wesley squeaked.

"He's got my ankles now," Moose reported. "Hang on." Moose's face was tomato red and sweat was beading on his forehead. We heard Moose grunt as Wesley grabbed his belt. Then Wesley must have found a foothold on the side of the drop-off and reached up to grab the same tree Moose was hanging on to. The two of them hung there panting.

Titus reached over the edge and grabbed Wesley. He pulled him over the side of drop-off. I grabbed Moose and did the same.

"Roll!" I yelled. The edge began to crumble and give way, but we rolled away in a clumsy pile and lay panting on the ground.

Wesley jumped to his feet. "Let's get out of here!"

"Wait," Titus yelled. "I want a picture of the cougar."

"Forget it," I told him. "Run!"

"No! Grab big sticks or branches," Meadow commanded.

We each hunted for something big, but light enough to carry.

"Why are we doing this?" I asked.

"We need to look big and tall so the cougar won't want to fight us. Now that we're away from her cubs, she'll probably leave us alone, but we need to watch our backs. We don't want her sneaking up on us. If she does follow us, you'll be glad for a weapon. And if she does show herself, don't run. Back away slowly."

I took her word for it. Meadow obviously knew lots more about cougar encounters than I did. We pushed our way over rocks and through trees. Every eye searched the area for trails or cougars. Every ear listened for danger. I couldn't help but think about Pastor Mac's sermon. People didn't call cougars ghost cats for nothing.

I glanced at my watch, and then checked it again. "Six o'clock! We've got to find that trail!"

"It's a good thing we live in western Montana," Titus said. "In summer I can read a newspaper outside at ten."

Wesley was limping. He must have twisted his ankle in the fall. We hadn't walked five minutes when rain came pouring down. We snuggled together under a dense stand of trees.

"Since when do you get pouring rain in August in Montana?" Moose asked. "Usually we're fighting forest fires this time of year."

Wesley sighed. "It's good to know that God is in control. He must have something in mind."

"He sure watched over you with the cougar," I pointed out.

"He did," Meadow agreed. "It's a good thing you're tall, Wesley. Cougars are much less likely to attack adults, especially tall people. The cougar was below you, and cougars would rather attack from above. You were with a group of people. Tana's rope helped. God made sure all of that came together to keep you safe. Some people don't even see a ghost cat until the cougar has leaped on them from behind, but God showed you she was there and helped you get away safely."

We stood silently watching the rain, feeling occasional drips, thanking God for our narrow escape. Forty minutes later the rain began to let up. Within minutes we found a strong path and started downhill. Our feet slid on rocks made slippery from the rain. Quick baby steps moved us down the trail.

I jolted to a stop. "Wait. Listen. I hear something."

Beep, beep, beep. Silence. *Beep, beep, beep.* It was a truck horn, very far away. Someone was looking for us.

We hurried faster down the hill. Wesley's limp became more noticeable. Then the path started an incline. Was this path leading us more downhill or up? Were we getting closer or farther away? At seven fifteen the horn sounded again, and then at seven thirty. Tana complained about her feet hurting, and Wesley admitted he just had to rest a minute. We sat on rocks beside the trail.

I looked at Titus. "You know its light at ten in western Montana in June. But it's mid-August now. We're in dense undergrowth on a very cloudy day. I don't think we have loads of light left."

Wesley decided his ankle had rested enough. We pushed on, picking our way more carefully over the trail in the waning light. The horn beeped at seven forty-five and eight o-clock. We were getting closer, but still had a long ways to go. Meadow led us, feeling her way more than seeing it.

The horn had just beeped at eight fifteen when Meadow jerked to a sudden halt. She pointed downward. "Look."

The five of us crept up to her and peeked down over a steep ledge.

"We're going to have to find shelter," I announced.

Wesley put his hands on his hips. "Shelter? We can't stay here overnight! What about the cougar?"

"What about *God is in control?*" Moose countered.

"If we keep walking, we're going to have another one of us down a drop-off and probably end up with a broken neck," I said. "Start hunting for shelter."

Meadow and Titus soon found a hollowed-out place in a rocky area. We gathered the driest pine needles we could find and formed a dry, soft floor for our overnight home.

Tana put on her jacket, now ripped where we had yanked the cords from it.

"Brrrr. It's getting kind of cold."

"It's gonna feel a lot colder than this before we're done," Titus said. "Do you have matches in that backpack of yours?"

Tana dug through her backpack. "Only wet ones. They fell in a puddle when we dumped my backpack."

Moose's face lit up then. "I've got a lighter."

We hollowed a fire pit and surrounded it with rocks. We were squinting into the darkness by the time we gathered a bit of firewood for the night. The six of us huddled together near the tiny fire.

Moose's stomach rumbled. "Hey, Tana. Got anything else to eat in that backpack?"

"Sorry. The granola bars were the last I had. I didn't expect to be on the mountain overnight."

"Too bad," Moose said. "Right now I'd be glad for those peanut butter sandwiches we spent all week earning."

Peanut butter sandwiches. Our prize for losing. Only now we weren't losing. We weren't even finishing.

Wesley rubbed his hands together by the crackling fire. "Well, y'all saved my skin today. Who knows? If you hadn't needed to stop and rescue me, we might have made it back to camp. Guess we'll have a cold night of it. Thanks for not leaving me in the woods. I know God is in control, but He chooses to use people, and I would have been in trouble without you guys. Y'all won't believe it, but I used to hunt squirrels in Tennessee?"

Moose snorted. "You? Sweet little Wesley W. Walters, hunt squirrels?"

"I did. My dad and I went. We didn't eat the meat ourselves, but we gave it to people who didn't have a lot of money. It was kind of for sport, but we did use the meat. Anyway, when Titus and Meadow were talking about shooting squirrels I didn't say anything because I didn't want to look bad, but there you are."

Moose added wood to the fire. "Well, I've been thinking about it, and I don't think I could shoot squirrels for sport anymore either."

"Me neither," I said.

Tana laughed. "You know how Pastor always asks for testimonies after camp? They'll wonder what kind of camp we went to. Everyone is going to go back home repenting of his hunting practices."

Titus shook his head. "Nothing wrong with that."

Silence hung over our tired little group. A coyote, a real one, howled in the distance. I reached for the cougar stick beside me. When one coyote quit yipping, another one started. Yet another joined them. The shrill wails joined together, each yip punctuating the next, blending into mournful harmony.

"The coyotes are singing a pretty song tonight," Meadow whispered. "It's a good thing there's plenty of deer this season. The cougar shouldn't give us any more problems now that we're far from her den and her cubs are safe."

It was Meadow's gentle way of reassuring everybody without acting like a know-it-all.

The coyotes took a break from singing. That made the other forest noises more noticeable. Owls hooted. Trees creaked. Something rustled the leaves. It made you wonder how big of an animal had passed and would grizzly bears really leave you alone if you left them alone?

After all our work that week I had hoped for better than freezing in the woods, lost, unable to even finish. Did we have anything to show for our week?

A horrific, piercing scream shattered my thoughts. My heart pounded. My hand clutched my cougar stick so tightly that the knuckles hurt. What could cause such a sound?

"It's a cougar's scream," Meadow whispered. Her voice was calm, but her cougar stick was near. "Sounds far away. I always wanted to hear one someday."

"Cool," Titus said. "I didn't get my picture, but I'll never forget a sound like that."

Tana scooted closer to the rest of the team. "Sounds creepy to me. Like demons screaming."

My heart still beat like a jackhammer. At this rate we'd be hysterical by morning. "Well, team," I said, "this hasn't exactly been an easy week. I don't really mind losing Eureka, but I would have liked to finish well. All the same, I think we ought to end our week with some memories. I want every person to name one funny thing that we will remember about this week."

Tana told how surprised she was when Moose picked her up and won the Bible illustration contest with Samson's riddle. Meadow admitted that, though she didn't laugh at the time, she thought it was hilarious when Wesley and Moose capsized in the kayak. Titus thought the picture of the team rescuing Wesley might win a photo award.

"So Cody, what did you find amusing about this week?" Wesley asked.

I thought a minute. "Well, sorry about this, Wesley. I didn't think it was funny at the time because I knew it would cause problems. But I've got to admit your skunk hair is pretty funny."

Wesley rubbed his hair, imagining the pale streak. "I guess. Too bad I lost my cap down the drop-off. Guess I'll have Mom dye my hair as soon as I get home. Then I'm going to tell the entire state of Montana that Moose's name is Malcolm Richards the third."

Moose mimicked Wesley meeting the skunk. Wesley stuck his tongue out at Moose. Tana started laughing. Then the whole exhausted mess of us caught the laughter, like a contagious disease. We talked about silly memories until we ran out of them. Then we sang camp choruses. Finally Meadow and Tana curled up with their backs together on their clump of pine needles. Soon Moose was snoring, and Wesley's head was nodding.

I decided to stay awake and watch for animals. I identified the various forest scents—pine and damp earth and smelly feet. I watched the fire die down. Forest sounds began to fade. My eyelids grew heavy. Only minutes later, it seemed, my eyes blinked open and rays of light filtered through the trees. I had drifted to sleep too. I counted my fellow Grizzlies. Five of them. Weren't there six? Oh, yes. I made six. No one had gotten eaten during the night.

"Hey, guys, it's morning," I whispered.

One by one each Grizzly shook himself awake. Everyone looked terrible.

"It's six o'clock. Dawn must have hit the other side of the mountain half an hour ago."

One by one they rose. Tana pulled out a mirror and brushed her hair. The guys visited the bushes on one side of our shelter and the girls the others. In five minutes we were stumbling down the trail. The more awake we became, the faster we went, though Wesley was limping a bit on his twisted ankle. Soon we heard honking—three short beeps and then a pause. Then three short beeps again. Sometime in the night they had given up signaling, but they were already starting again. I could just imagine how worried they were when we didn't show up the night before.

"They're looking for us!" I said. "They'll have vehicles with them. We can catch a ride back to camp and get a good breakfast."

We sped up. Wesley lagged behind. His pinched face showed that his leg was killing him.

"Come on, Moose, let's help him out," I said. Wesley put one arm high over Moose's shoulder and one arm low over mine. We worked out a rhythm, kind of like a three-legged race, until we were moving pretty fast. Forty-five minutes brought us to the parking area. There Pastor Mac and Dr. Walters stood, gazing up the trail. When they saw us, they took blankets from the truck and ran toward us.

We each grabbed a blanket and wrapped up.

"Are you all right?" Dr. Walters asked.

Wesley nodded. "Yes, sir."

"Where were you?"

Wesley shrugged. "It's hard to say exactly."

"What did you do to your leg?"

Wesley grinned. "Aw, you know me. Always the klutz. But lucky for me—no, fortunately—wait. That's not right either. Good friends are God's blessing, and I'd be lost without my teammates."

I told them that we had gotten slightly lost and had technical difficulties. We'd be glad for a ride back to camp.

Moose interrupted me. "Nah. If we get a ride back to camp, we're quitters. Eureka rules say you have to walk back on your own. We may be thirteen hours late and lose thirteen thousand points, but we are going to finish. I may be a loser, but I'm not a quitter. We're going to walk in together and finish well. Isn't that right, Wesley?"

"Gotta earn our peanut butter sandwiches," he said.

It sounded crazy, but I knew we'd lose a lot more than the game if we quit now. "Come on, guys. Let's go."

Moose set his cowboy hat on Wesley's head, covering the skunk hair. Then he and I got back into position with Wesley between us.

Dr. Walters wrapped a blanket around the three of us. He stood, still and silent, until Wesley's eyes met his. "I feel like Samuel Wesley," he whispered.

Wesley grinned.

Then Dr. Walters caught my eye. He smiled. "Thanks."

Pastor Mac pulled the keys to his truck out of his pocket. "We'll drive back to camp and let everyone know you're all right."

The pastors drove off and we started walking.

I told Moose, "Just remember this was your idea. No one else would be crazy enough to suggest we turn down a ride at a time like this."

Moose focused on our legwork, working to keep the rhythm. "I may be crazy, but I'm not going to quit. When I get to camp I'm going to demand my peanut butter sandwich. And I'm going to scrub those toilets if it kills me."

We fell silent then. Half a mile is a long way to walk when you are hungry and exhausted and minus a walking leg. We lined up side by side determined to walk into camp as a team.

A truck passed us on the road. A dog ran down a drive and barked as we passed.

We passed a tree house with a pink roof. Tana grinned. "See? Pink."

We rounded the last turn, and there by the gate stood all the campers, the counselors, even the cooks. Out in front stood Luke grinning. He was sure to give us a hard time. We not only lost; we lost big time.

Then Luke pointed to the pillowcase flying on the flagpole. "Cody is champ!" it said. Luke shook his fist in the air. "Woo hoo!" he shouted.

Everyone started yelling, actually cheering. As we walked to the finish line all the voices were lifted in one gigantic cheer. "Go Grizzlies!"

We all grinned. We didn't feel like losers anymore.